And there before us lay . . . **Ilionis!**

It was old, that city; old and dead. Ages beyond
the numbering of man had trampled it down
into the dust. The once-proud walls lay fallen in
huge sections. The houses and mansions were
empty, gutted black windows leering like the
eye-sockets of hollow skulls. Sand had drifted,
grain by grain, into the silent streets, until they
were carpeted with dust.

All of red marble was lost and ruined Ilionis, and
the centuries had cracked and pitted and
splintered that dead stone to crumbling ruins.
The broken towers and fallen rubble lay ghostly
before us in the dim light of the dying day, and
it well may be that no living eyes had looked
on Ilionis for millions of years, until our
coming. . . .

The Man Who Loved Mars

Lin Carter

WILDSIDE PRESS

THE MAN WHO LOVED MARS

THE MAN WHO LOVED MARS
is for Isaac Asimov, Lester Del Rey,
George O. Smith, and the rest of
my friends in my favorite club,
The Trap-Door Spiders.

Contents

The Man Who Loved Mars

1. Ivo Tengren

Lilac and violet and velvety purple, the arcade lies drowned in shadows where I sit in the late afternoon, sipping resinous brandy, the murmurous, familiar litany of the shoeshine boys coming toward me as they drift among the tables, blending with the curdled, plaintive moaning of plump, breathless pigeons waddling in the sun.

Beyond the arcade the plaza of San Pietro lies stunned in the blinding day, a pool of motionless white light. The cheap brandy bites my tongue, tart and heavy. I shake my head to the boy who pauses inquiringly before my table, and he moves on to the next tourist.

The bells of the old and hideous cathedral break into their jangled thunder, saluting the hour. All the pigeons rise from the sun-soaked tiles in the same instant, as if galvanized by the cacophonous cadence of the bells that they have heard all their brief lives and yet somehow have never become accustomed to. In a great startled cloud, a snowstorm of black confetti, they swoop up, flapping from the square, and swing in a loose, revolving astronomy of black motes, wheeling around the pink stucco spires of the cathedral where four bird-limed saints stare without expression over the red rooftops of Venice.

I drained the last drop of the brandy and set the tumbler down with a click on the wrought-iron table and pulled a crumpled pack of aromatiques out of the pocket of my sweat-stained shirt. Selecting one, I sucked on it until the tip ignited.

A noisy group of American tourists entered the cool, shadow-drowned arcade. Coming into the purple gloom of the arcade from the brilliance of the sun-lit street beyond, where heat settled in dusty layers on the worn old stones like volcanic ash, they were struck by the difference and

11

found it enormously comic. One of them, a fat man of fifty or so, with a very expensive depth camera slung around his red neck, went stumbling around, bumping into tables in a pantomime of blindness that sent the frowsy females of the group into paroxysms of mirth. At length, with a noisy clatter of iron chairs, they settled themselves, calling loudly for a waiter.

I turned around to catch the waiter's eye and pointed an eloquent thumb at my empty tumbler. He nodded to me . . . and then a small wintry wind began blowing up my spine.

Two men had entered the cool gloom of the arcade behind the Americans. I got a good look at them when I turned to signal the waiter. One was youngish, mid-thirties, tall and husky and handsome in a dark, coarse, Slavic sort of way. He wore a gray suit of shiny kyrolan with black, wet patches under the arms. I only caught a quick glimpse of him as I turned back: beefy neck, swarthy face, short, neatly trimmed black beard, and cold hard eyes like the points of gimlets.

He spotted me and grabbed his companion's arm. The other one peered at me. He was older, perhaps in his sixties, with a gaunt gentleman's face, tanned and leathery, and a beautiful head of silver hair.

I pretended not to have noticed, and I don't think they saw that I had spotted them, for I turned away from my waiter-fetching in one smooth motion and sat there with my back to them, my heart drumming, and a cold despair settling like lead in the depths of my gut. After all that time it still got me hard. But I should be used to it.

I sat and smoked and stared at nothing, and the small cold wind was still blowing up my spine . . . Still, what did I have to fear from the rotten swine after all these years? They have done all they could do to me, taken everything I own from me. My purpose, my people, my livelihood, friends, even my self-respect. Everything. Except my life. *Except my life . . .*

But that was arrant nonsense! They could have had that too, along with all the rest, years ago when I was still kicking feebly between the jaws of the courts and the grasping claws of the lawyers. When they brought me back from Mars in the Mandate craft, I fully expected the death penalty. And even if they were afraid of doing it in the full eye of the press and the public, I knew full well one of the crack Colonial Administration assassination teams could have picked me off after the trial and the publicity died down, and no one would have cared. No. I have nothing to fear from them anymore.

So I sat and sweated and stretched out my legs, trying to relax the muscles that kept tensing for action. I crushed out the butt and ignited another aromatique, pulling the tobacco-flavored, noncarcinogenic smoke deep down into my lungs, enjoying the mild bite and letting it out slowly. I stared at the sun-drenched Piazza del San Pietro, where the pigeons settled down to earth again, to waddle and bob and cluck and coo their meandering way over the shimmering tiles, undisturbed until the next hour and the next explosion of the cathedral bells. *Let them watch, if they like,* I thought to myself without emotion. *I have done nothing; there is nothing they can do to me anymore . . .*

The waiter brought my drink on a small black plastic tray, gathering up a damp collection of currency, and padded away, slippers flopping, bearing off the empty glass. I smoked and sipped the tart brandy and watched the lilac shadows lengthen from the old arcade and soak the plaza's steaming tiles in their pools of stagnant purple. *Are they still watching? I will not turn and look . . .*

I tried to regain the mood of somnolence and comfort, but it would not come.

For some reason my mind drifted to the great stone lion, the winged lion of marble, brought here in the twilight of the seventeenth century from the Piraeus near Athens; the Winged Lion of St. Mark that is at once the guardian, the emblem, and the genius of Venice. I thought too of the neat lines of runes carved upon it, the inscription cut in the worn old stone nearly a thousand years ago by the hands of Viking warriors somehow strayed from their cold fjords to the crystalline bays of Greece:

> They cut him down in the midst of his force
> but in the harbour the men cut runes
> in memory of Horsa, a good warrior, by the sea.
>
> The Swedes set this on the lion.
>
> He went his way with good counsels
> gold he won in his travels.
>
> The warriors cut runes   coloured them
> in memory of Horsa.
>
> He won gold in his travels.

Musing on the old runic verse, I wondered if the people have composed such an obituary to my memory as well. . . . If so, perhaps it is not so very different from the lines Horsa's comrades cut to commemorate his fall. Save that I won no gold in my travels. Only an empire that I neither deserved nor wanted nor could defend. And memories that burn like iron and cut like fire.

A clatter behind me in the depths of the old arcade. Shadows were lengthening; evening neared; the sky reddened. The waiters were coming now with their tight, shiny black trousers and swarthy faces blending into the gathering dusk and only their startlingly white jackets visible in the gloom. One by one they moved the flimsy wrought-iron tables and chairs from under the arcade into the warm plaza. It was time for me to finish my drink and go, back to my cramped, dusty little flat up two flights of flimsy stairs in the hostel by the small side canal, where I had lived now for most of a year.

Soon, with evening, the plaza of the old cathedral would be transformed into an open-air café. Strings of bulbs in faded Japanese lanterns of tinted paper. Colored lights. The old fountain playing, its glimmering jets laving the sleek green thighs of the bronze nymph and the beard of the kneeling satyr, who have stood for more than two centuries in uneasy proximity to the pink stucco home of the bird-limed saints, a weird dichotomy, this juxtaposition of faded paganism and stiff Catholicism. A whisper of cool breeze off the bay would set the paper lanterns bobbing. And I would be here again with evening. Watching the crowd and drinking bad Chianti with my cheap meal, watching the young lovers, two by two, leaning across the small tables toward each other, hands plaited together on white cloth, the candles between them guttering behind glass, dividing them each from the other and bathing their faces, their young eager faces, in a soft, restless, romantic glow . . . *and I would think of Yakla with silver beads woven through the silk of her hair, the first time I saw her in the back alleys of Syrtis, her eyes like wet black jewels, the pure oval of her dusky face bathed in the intermittent glare of the landing jets of a satellite shuttle from Deimos Station . . .Yakla, Yakla! Kitten soft and tigress fierce, warm in the shadow of my arms, weaving her long hair up after love, her voice like liquid silver as she sang an old Drylands love ode . . . Yakla, who died horribly under the beta guns that night they broke our charge by the walls of ancient Niophar . . .* Heaven and earth, must I remember?

"Citizen, pardon me. Aren't you Ivo Tengren?"

Almost I had managed to forget them, when the low voice spoke from behind my chair. I turned not too swiftly and saw that there were three of them now: the saintly old gentleman with the weathered face and beautiful silvery hair; the big burly Slavic tough who had (I now noticed) a greasy skin and coarse pores; and a girl, stiff and starched and blond as summer wheat. She had a curious air about her, a way of looking obliquely at things, as if she highly disapproved of everything. I disliked her on sight, almost as much as I distrusted the big man with the sweat stains under his arms.

"I am." I kept my voice cold and neutral and my face without expression. "It has been quite a while, gentlemen, since we had one of these little visits. You will be wanting to see my visa. It is in my flat; but it has not yet expired, as you can find out from the——"

"Ah . . . I think that you have us confused with some-one else . . . I'm quite sure we have never met." It was the

old man who spoke. His voice was cultured, almost courtly.

I said nothing, did nothing, merely sat relaxed and
watched him: waiting. He flushed, and then his face
brightened.

"Oh, I think I understand . . . You are mistaken, Cn.
Tengren, we are *not* from the political force. You must
forgive me if I gave any such impression."

"Then what do you want with me?" I asked. "If you are
news people, I'm certain I must long since have ceased
being copy."

"Here, let me—" the big man said but his older
comrade laid a frail gnarled hand on his arm and said, "I
will do the talking, Bolgov." The other subsided, and the
quiet-voiced old man made a little half-bow to me and
broke into the most charming smile.

"No, not news men either, Citizen! Merely, ah, private
travelers like yourself. Permit me to make introductions. I
am Dr. Josip Keresny, formerly of the Luna City Museum. My pilot and associate, Cn. Konstantin Bolgov.
And my granddaughter Ilsa . . . I wonder if we might join
your table for a few moments, to discuss a business ar-
rangement which would be mutually advantageous?"

I didn't feel in the mood for company, and besides, that
chill little wind of apprehension was still whispering up my
spine. But before I could think of anything to say, they
took my silence for consent and sat down. We looked at
each other in awkward silence for a moment, all except for
the old man's granddaughter, who was still ignoring the
whole matter in her cool, irritating way. More or less for
want of anything else to say, I remarked, "Josip Keresny.
Keresny. Polish?" He shook his head with another of
those utterly charming smiles.

"No, Citizen. Yugoslav, although I was raised in Lon-
don. My father was a minister in the Exile Regime after
the Second Counterrevolution of '74."

"My mother was a Yugoslav," I remarked idly. "From
somewhere around Zagorje, I think, although I haven't the
faintest idea where Zagorje is."

"Zagorje! Why, my people—"

"Can't we get on with it, Josip?" the big man growled. What was his name again?

"Kostantin Bolgov, was it?" I mused. "That sounds Russian . . ." I didn't give a damn where they were from: why was I drawing this out—who was I trying to needle?

The Doctor, like most old people, was animated on the subject of family backgrounds. "Close, close, Cn. Tengren! But not quite, no, Konstantin here, his people are from the Ukraine, but he was raised in Paris, I believe; his family were ousted during the Time of Troubles too. . . . And you, I believe, are a West German?"

I nodded. "True. And raised in exile as well. We're quite a little group of second-generation refugees, aren't we?" I said sardonically. "A pocket version of the Associated Nations, in fact. We should get together and issue a White Paper or something."

My feeble attempt at humor sounded pretty lame even to my own ears, but the Doctor laughed as heartily as if I were a famed stereo comic or someone of comparable glittering wit. Bolgov growled something under his breath (which was redolent of garlic, I could not help noticing) and cracked his knuckles with a sickening sound. The Doctor, now that we were on jovial grounds with the social amenities out of the way, tried to flag down a waiter without success. But Ilsa was getting restive.

"Please, Grandfather, Konstantin's right. Get on with it," she said in a pained voice that had the high-bred tones one acquires only in one of those expensive Swiss finishing schools for young gentlewomen.

So we got down to business.

"As I told you, Cn. Tengren, I was formerly associated with the Luna City Museum," the old man said.

"That's right, so you did, but you forgot to mention in what capacity."

"Extraterrestrial archeology is my field," he said.

"Which means Mars, I assume, unless the Lunarian *Arachnidae* have a culture somewhat higher than the science newscasts credit them with." He nodded, smiling at my words. With a smile as gracious and warm as his, he was wasting himself in XT archeology; he belonged in the diplomatic corps.

"You're right, of course, High **Martian** is my area. I am more of a research man than a field archeologist, I am afraid, although I have made two extended visits to the planet. The most recent was during your . . . ah . . ." I was wrong, he would be disastrous in diplomacy. I couldn't help smiling as he fumbled for an inoffensive term; I finally supplied him with a rude one.

"During my war of revolution?" I offered sardonically. He flushed unhappily and then nodded, white locks wobbling seraphically.

"Ah, ah, yes, I suppose one could call it that," he said in a flustered tone. "Well, at any rate, during my dig near the Thoth-Nepenthes canal complex to the south of Isidis Regio, I was fortunate enough to come upon a veritable treasure trove of Late Dynastic artifacts, including some subelectronic specimens of Early technology—"

I lifted my brows questioningly. "Near *Thoth-Nepenthes?* Hard to believe. The Nine Nations never got north of the Mare Tyrrhenum until way after the Late Period, according to their own sagas—"

He shook his head helplessly. "I know! That's what makes it so incredible; but there is not the slightest doubt as to the era. Wait, wait, you have yet to hear the truly important news—" Dr. Keresny's voice dropped to low, solemn tones, which trembled with excitement.

"The most important find of all was clear, precise directions to *the Lost City of Ilionis!*" he announced portentously.

There came an interval of silence; they looked at my face, even the girl, to note my reaction.

I *laughed!*

I had not laughed so in years, heartily, loudly, without restraint—or bitterness. I whooped with mirth until the tears ran down my face. The Doctor looked foolish, slack jawed. The blond girl looked pained, as if her refined sensibilities were offended by my rude hilarity. Konstantin Bolgov glowered, his big hands curling into thick fists. I think I may have prolonged my bellows of laughter just a little,' to provoke him. But I could not help it . . . Ilionis, fabled Ilionis, the long-lost and extremely legended Treasure City of Old Mars, goal of every prospector, treasure hunter, fortune seeker, and adventurer that ever stepped off the satellite shuttle from Deimos Station! It was delicious. There must be fifty thousand bogus treasure maps circulating around the stews and back alleys of Sun Lake City and Yeolarn and Syrtis, and every one shows the route to the Lost City. Not a booze-soaked bum in the wine shops of the twelve colonies but has a special, infallible clue to the whereabouts of the Lost City, which he will reveal for a few beakers of fiery *chardaka*. For all his scholarship the learned Doctor was as gullible as the greenest tourist fresh off a Trans-Planet liner on his first tour. He couldn't have gotten halfway to his hotel before being offered a true, exact, original Old High Dynasty map which revealed the hiding place of the long-lost treasure city!

My mirth finally faded out in chuckles. The old fellow regarded me in a stiff, rather shocked, and disapproving manner that showed me where his granddaughter got the syndrome. I wiped my eyes on the soiled cuff of my travelalls. And I was about to say something more or less polite and very final, before bidding them a last adieu and ambling back to my flat, when Bolgov did it.

He kicked back his chair and started to rise, hot black eyes boiling with vicious temper, growling, "I tol' you this was a waste of time! Maybe you want to sit here and listen to this broken-down, Cat-lovin' old wino laugh in your face, but not me! I got better things to do with my time."

There was a silence, in which I could feel my face grow stiff and hot. My heart thudded, and my hand trembled just a little, rattling the tumbler.

Cat-lover . . .

I had heard those words before. Many times.

They hung there in the cool, shadowy, late afternoon air, echoing in my ears. Then I relaxed, as if the tension was over, as if a decision had been reached. And a vast and exhilarating joy welled up within me, rising from the depths of me and went tingling through my veins. I rose to my feet very swiftly, a joyous grin on my face, and braced myself before Bolgov quite realized what I was doing.

Then I planted one balled fist right in the pit of his stomach with everything I had in my back, shoulder, and arm. And followed through with a honey of a left that caught him on the side of the bearded jaw with a beautiful, meaty smack. It was superb.

He went over backward, legs tangling with the wrought-iron chair in a terrible clatter and flurry of kicking feet, landing full on his shoulders. I stood there and watched him groggily spew the contents of his stomach all over that handsome suit of gray kyrolan and felt a vast inner contentment such as I had not known for many, many months. We ex-monarchs, though deposed, have our pride. We rarely get a chance to show it so pleasantly.

I made a small bow to the Doctor and the girl, both of whom were frozen with the suddenness of the thing.

"Thank you for a delightful conversation," I said lightly. "A pity it has to terminate in such a very physical way. However, I am not in the least interested in investing in any treasure maps to the Lost City, thank you. They are half a dozen to the dollar in any of the better bazaars anywhere in Sun Lake City. I am not interested. Good evening!"

And I turned grandly on my heel to make my way through the tables. But the Doc was quicker on the uptake than I would have thought. He uttered eight words in a quiet voice that stopped me dead in my tracks.

"Not interested in a free ticket to Mars?"

I stood there and felt the ache rise up within me, who could never legally go off-planet for the rest of my days. . . . It had been the price of my freedom, so-called: permanent, life-long revocation of my off-planet visa. I was glad my back was turned so they could not see the expression on my face.

And then the old man clinched it, and I was lost.

"It's not a treasure map, Cn. Tengren," he said softly, very softly. "It was a *thought record* that I found there in the ruins near Thoth-Nepenthes."

I think I forgot to breathe for a while. I know that suddenly my chest ached and blood was roaring in my ears. A thought record! They could not be faked. Nor forged. Nor imitated. Only the mysterious savants of the Ancients knew the strange art of indelible mind recordings—*iophotha*, they call them in the High Tongue. There have only been two of them discovered in all the three-quarters of a century that terrestrial man has been on Mars, and they are beyond price. If he had a genuine thought record . . .

"Start talking," I said, as I turned around and took my seat again.

2. An Hour Before Earthrise

All my life I have taken the most obvious route to the things I wanted, and with unfailing accuracy this has led me into the most obvious pitfalls. Often I have wanted to make myself over, dreamed of being a subtle, devious man, full of shrewdness and cunning, but the gods did not mold me of such clay. Of course, I was an idealist, a young reckless fool, and of course, I dreamed the old humanitarian dreams of "love thy neighbor" and all the rest of it. When I went to Mars ten years before, a wise man could have predicted almost everything that was going to happen to me: but there I was, a dreamy boy, eyes filled with starry hopes, heart drunk on high ideals that had gone out of fashion generations before, a young sociotician, a student of the ancient indigenous civilization of that dim, far-off, age-old desert world. It was the most natural thing in the world that I should be shaken and disgusted by the callous inhumanity and naked greed and terracentric contempt with which the Colonial Administration treated a people whose dignity and graciousness and lonely pride were all they had left of a magnificent civilization that had already begun to die while our own ancestors still slunk or slithered through the steamy fens of the Paleozoic . . .

Of course, I could not resist the old man's offer. The plan was simplicity itself, and as for the offer, it was irresistible. For—how many years was it now? Only two?—I had dreamed of nothing else. *"A free ticket to Mars . . ."* I would gladly have paid any price, were it possible for me to buy my way back to that dim red world that fate or chance or fortune had made my heart's home. But that could never be. No liner would carry me, no ticket agent would accept my fare, no visa could be obtained; I was like one of the old sailors back in the distant days of sailing ships—marooned for the unforgivable crime, the ultimate sin against a society I had come to loathe. *Mutiny.*

The only difference was that in my case they had chosen my desert island with exquisite cruelty: for I was an exile on the planet of my birth, my body's homeland, my spirit's prison. And now an old man's avarice or lust for fame or whatever it was offered me a way out. A way home.

It all came out over coffee and cigars and a Lunarian liqueur I had never tasted before and whose name I have forgotten. The plaza before the old cathedral was a bit too public; I went back to their hotel, to the private suite Keresny had taken for the week. The suite was in one of the towers of The Grand Canal; this had been the newest of Venice's innumerable hotels, a big, dull, Kremlin-style edifice the Russians had put up in the eighties during their transitory dream of world empire. It had been the administration center of all this part of Italy. After that particular dream crashed to ruin in the fire shower of the Twenty-Nine-Minute War, the Italians reclaimed it, knocked off the Ivan-the-Terrible gingerbread, dynamited the onion-shaped domes, and turned it into a first-class hotel. Today it was dingy, smelling of mildew and rat dung, slumping into decay.

Before we got down to the talking, the girl, Ilsa, drew the soundproof curtains while the greasy-faced Ukrainian, favoring me all the while with surly, glowering looks, unpacked a slim plastic case from the mound of luggage and

set it going. I cocked a thumb at the gadget and raised an inquiring eyebrow.

"Is all well, Konstantin?" the Doctor asked, before answering my unspoken query. The surly Russian growled assent.

"Merely a slight precaution, Cn. Tengren. I believe the Americans, in their delightful slang, call it a debugging device. We have no particular reason to believe our rooms are under electronic surveillance; still, one can never be sure in these troubled times. And rumor has it that most hotels these days tape everything that happens on their premises as a matter of course. I believe some of the less scrupulous of them make a tidy sum giving information to the government spies and the political police."

"It's been a national custom for years," I grinned. "Won't they be suspicious, though, when this room registers a blank tape?"

He smiled that saintly smile again. "Not at all; almost everyone uses one of these devices. They are easily available on the Gray Market and most reasonably priced. Spies and criminals and revolutionaries—but also ordinary businessmen with an important contract to negotiate and everyday people cheating on their wives—use them. The instrument merely broadcasts a heterodyne wave that oscillates all over the radio frequencies, quite effectively scrambling the sound recordings. Since the wave is continuously overlapping, and the oscillations are purely random, it is technologically impossible to unscramble the tapes. But come! Let's to business. My dear, coffee, I think, unless Cn. Tengren would prefer brandy . . . ?"

"I've had enough for one night, I think."

He offered me the best cigar I had tasted in six years; I leaned back in the big, comfortable pneumochair. It adjusted its shape to the contours of my body and began unobtrusively massaging the back of my neck and the muscles of my shoulders. I drank in the richly mellow smoke and let the old man talk in his smooth, gentlemanly diplomat voice, while the girl took the surly Ukrainian off somewhere to fix his face; he came back with his purpled jaw repaired with cosmetic gel above the beard and his vom-

it-messed suit exchanged for electric blue lounging paja-
mas. He looked a lot better, but from the smouldering
glances he shot at me from time to time, I knew his temper
had not improved. That sort of muscular lout protects
his masculine self-image by throwing his weight around. I
had hit him directly in the virility center of his ego—a far
more sensitive spot than the pit of his stomach—and he
would not soon forget that I had made him look ridiculous
in the presence of the blond girl. I would have trouble with
that one, I knew. But I hardly cared: if they could get me
to Mars, they could break every bone in my body.

"Just a precaution," the Doctor was saying in that beautiful, soothing voice. "I quite doubt if the politicals are still
watching you after all this while; perhaps an occasional
spot check, nothing more. But it's been two full years
since, ah, since your legal troubles, and even the publicity
must have died down long since. With the instrument on,
we are safe from anything outside of an audio search
beam, and you will observe I have seated our little group
out of any possible direct beam, and the curtains should
muffle our little conversation. Better to be on the safe
side . . ."

The only question I asked, at the start, was the obvious
one. If he had a thought record that told the way to the
fabulous Treasure City, why did he need me? I told him,
not quite with complete candor—but I'll get back to that
later—that I knew no more than most people about Lost
Ilionis.

"Ah, but that is the simplest of all questions to answer,
my dear sir!" he said in his quaint and charming, courtly
way. "We will be going deep into the Drylands, far deeper
than any—what is it they call us? *F'yagh?* Outworlder?—
has ever gone before. You know as well as I that beyond
the Drylands we will be getting into High Clan country: a
proud people; an ancient people; they have never yielded
to the authority of the Colonial Administration, and they
have never ratified the Great Treaty—"

"Why should they, since the CA cops never got close
enough to them to hold a gun to the heads of their
women? Which is the way the bastards got the rest of the

Nations to sign that piece of toilet paper." The bitterness
locked up in my guts for so long must have leaked into my
tone of voice, for the old man favored me with a gently
commiserating smile and uttered some soothing platitude
about the nobility of patriotism and hurried on to spread a
little goose grease on my ego.

"We stand no chance of getting into that country without being stopped by High Clan war patrols, and that is
where your services will prove completely indispensable,"
he said.

"I don't know about that; they have never seen me; they
may not even have heard the news that an Outworlder has
the Iron Crown."

His eyes twinkled benignly, but he was unswerving.
"You know how to prove to even the Wild Huntsmen who
you are," he said gently.

He had me there.

"All right, we get by them. But do you really believe the
warriors of the High Clans will let even me lead a party of
Hated Ones into the Treasure City—the most sacred place
on the whole of the planet?"

The benign twinkle did not even flicker. "Your whim is
a holy law from Syrtis to the Pole," he said. "With the
Jamad Tengru at our head, why, we could ride across the
Bridge of Fire to the very gates of Yhoom, the Hidden
World of the Gods, without fear or hindrance. Without
you in our midst we would not get ten meters beyond the
River of Death."

He had me there too. The full scope of my authority
had seldom been brought home to me with so vivid an il-
lustration. A billion years of Holy Law encloaked me: my
person was sacrosanct: my mere word could open gates
locked two hundred million years. At my whim ten thousand warriors would ride into the gaping jaws of hell . . .
again, as very often in the wild, warring years gone by, I
quailed beneath the awful burden that had been be-
queathed to me. And the taste of my unworthiness was
like brass upon my tongue.

Dr. Keresny sensed my mood of depression with the
faultless tact of a born diplomat. He rose, went over to a

coffee table, fetched back a liqueur flask and three glasses. The oily fluid, which he identified as Lunarian, was amber-colored, smooth on the tongue, with a musky, mushroomy taste and a heart of golden fire. Doubtless the *Arachnidae* extracted it from some slimy fungus in their lightless caverns: I did not care. It was heady, strong, with a real bite to it. I leaned back in the chair and let him talk. Gradually, I relaxed, letting the liqueur, the espresso, and the superb Panatella work their old white magic, letting the chair work out the tension at the nape of my neck, idly listening to his roundabout conversational style, watching his granddaughter. She was indeed pleasant on the eyes: tall, cool as iceberg lettuce, blond as summer wheat, with a long, lithe, lovely pair of legs revealed from crotch to toe in a silky sheath of iolon. She wore one of the currently fashionable peekaboo blouses, certain portions of which became completely transparent at random intervals, and during one of those random intervals I could hardly help noticing that she had superb breasts, tanned, firm, deliciously tip-tilted, and they looked natural. Still, you can never tell, and the marvels of cosmetic plastisurgery are cheap enough these days. But she amused me by her manner: despite her fashionably provocative bodyglove she was prim as a school marm. She sat stiffly erect, not allowing herself to relax in the lascivious embrace of the pneumo; and she sat with her sleek, lovely knees pressed primly together. In fact, her entire body, stiff, awkwardly erect, tight, made me wonder if it was possible she could be a virgin. In these hectic days, with complete permissiveness a universal lifestyle, it seemed hardly possible. She must have been eighteen at least, perhaps twenty, but no more.

It might be amusing to find out, I thought.

The plan was so completely simple it might well work. The museum had kept an old Icarus under charter for many years; the AN Space Mandate, of course, made it highly illegal for any individual or organization to actually "own" any kind of spacecraft—they could be chartered by reputable corporations for provably legal purposes, but the charter was reviewed periodically and could be revoked in a second. This was one of the many clever little ways the AN had thus far kept any nasty little wars from cropping up in this Brave New Century.

The Doctor had retired from the museum staff, but he had not completely severed relations, for he was still on the rolls as a sort of emeritus. It had not been hard for him to lease the old Icarus from the museum for a little private expedition of his own. Nor to hire my sweaty friend with the bruised jaw as his pilot. The Icarus was in docking orbit around Luna, and we could be aboard by dawn, since the Doctor had a last year's Lanzetti parked on the roof of the hotel and was set to check out this evening. There was simply no problem; no one would notice me as I accompanied them to the parking roof, and even if they did, they could hardly know who or what I was. There was no reason why a Mandate patrol should intercept the Lanzetti on its flight to the moon, providing the Doc kept to the right lane; and no particular reason why the Mandate should single out for scrutiny a rusty old tub of an Icarus as it broke out of docking orbit bound for Mars. It was perfection itself. With only one slight snag.

"And what is that, my friend?"

I inhaled another drop of the rare Lunarian liqueur before answering. "Me. They don't keep me under regular surveillance—or at least, I don't *think* they do: I've been a good boy for two years, and all I've done is warm an endless succession of bar stools and café chairs, nursing my growing reputation as a seedy, down-at-heels, lachrymose, middle-aging failure. More than a bit of a wino, as Konstantin would say, and did, to his regrets. But the woman who rents me my room will know when I don't come home—I owe her this month's rent—and she will go to the police. They will comb every gutter in Venice, and surely Luigi—my pet waiter—will remember the trio of tourists who spoke to me at my table this afternoon and who left with me. Luigi has an eye like a camera; he'll give a detailed description of the three of you, and then all the police have to do is to cross-check those descriptions against the pictures of you people; perhaps you are not familiar with the routine, but the customs officials make photocopies of the identity pictures in every visitor's visa, just for the files. By this time tomorrow noon they will have everything they need, including the flight plan of your Icarus. And the Mandate patrols will be right there when we approach docking orbit around Mars. I hate to let unpleasant facts intrude like this, but—"

I broke off because the strong-arm lug with the bruised jaw was grinning toothily through his black bush of beard and I saw a flash of cool amusement in the contemptuous eyes of the girl.

"Please do not trouble yourself," the old man smiled. "I rather pride myself on having considered all facets of this affair and let me ease your mind by saying at once that you are *already* home—you got there about twenty minutes ago."

The bewildered expression on my face must have been a singularly stupid-looking one, because Konstantin growled out a grunting laugh. Then the old man dug into his attaché case and presented me with a plain manila envelope, the eight-by-ten size that professional modeling agencies use to hold glossies. I dug into it and drew out a sheaf of expensive depth photos. They were of me. Good likenesses too. The only trouble was that I could not recall having posed for them.

Looking a bit closer, I saw the discrepancies. That lump of scar tissue on the bridge of my nose, a small souvenir from the time the Colonial cops had "interrogated" me, was not quite the same coffee color as my Italian Riviera tan. It was plasmoid, the kind of professional stage make-up actors use to simulate a broken nose. And the set of the shoulders was a bit too jaunty to successfully imitate my weary slump. But the hairline was perfect, and the eyes were good, very good. Even the mouth.

"The cinema industry has died here since the center of world filmmaking made one of its periodic moves, this time, I believe, to Pan-India. It was not difficult to locate a specimen of your physical type from the local equivalent of central casting, or to hire the actor without a formal contract, which would demand registry with the unions. He speaks his Italian with just your kind of a German accent, and as he once played Cristoffsen in a local film epic, he knows how to walk with a—what is it you call it?"

"A Mars shuffle," I supplied the term. I felt a little numb. The Doc had, in fact, thought of everything. There was no real excuse I could find for backing out of this . . . not that I wanted to, I told myself fiercely . . . or did I? I wanted to be alone, to examine my feelings, but there was no time for that, no leisure to contemplate the alternatives or count the chances against failure. The Doctor wanted to leave within the hour: it was now or never. And I knew this was my last chance. My only chance. That one-in-a-billion chance I had dreamed about all these past two years.

Perhaps the old man took my lapse into brooding silence for suspicion. Anyway, he spoke up in that soothing voice of his that could have made his fortune in the diplomatic corps.

"You needn't be afraid that I have brought any unseen partners in to finance this expedition, my friend. My retirement pension is very adequate to one of my spartan requirements. And I have recorded a few textbooks in my time that bring in a surprising royalty twice each year. We coached the actor all week long in your habits and drinking tastes; he was eager to get work, and he was not expensive. After a week or ten days he will pack up and go to Milan, and there he will drop out of sight and resume his own identity. There is a registered package for him at the express office in Milan, but he can not pick it up until the seventeenth of the month. Oh, they will know you have eluded them but not right away. We will have vanished into the hinterlands of Mars long before the police realize you cannot be found: trust me, my friend. I have as much to lose, should we fail in this endeavor, as do you."

I chewed it over, and it tasted good. But still . . .

"Your actor looks good, damn good, I'll admit. He would fool the average storekeeper or gondola jockey, who knows me enough to say *buon giorno*. But he isn't good enough to fool someone who sees and talks to me every day, and he'll run a gauntlet of plenty of those: the kid that bring me my *New York Times-Post-News* every morning, the old woman in the market who sells me rolls and sausage, my landlady—or the waiter who serves me my brandy every afternoon—"

"Probably not; but he won't have to. This evening you are going to develop a terrible toothache. You will bandage your jaw and growl curtly to your landlady and keep to your bed very much of the time: the street boy that brings you your newsfax will run your errands for you and will innocently spread the word of your discomforture. Really, Cn. Tengren, you must trust me. I have anticipated everything."

"Not quite. There are a few mementos I would rather not be parted from and at least one item which I will need on Mars—"

I broke off as he smiled again that saintly, beaming smile and dipped into the attaché case to bring out precisely those of my few belongings I would not want to have left behind. They were nothing much, a battered Everyman copy of Dowson, an old pre-Troubles Loeb edition of Quintus Smyrnaeus, and the antique Tauchnitz Shakespeare I had carried everywhere since school. I fingered the things absently, the depth photo of my mother and father and brother, and the little portrait-bust of Yakla that the old sorcerer had delicately carved out of *slidar* ivory for me that tenday we hid from the CA skimmers in the ruins of Ygnarh.

And the crown itself, of course.

I did not unwrap it from its place in the folds of the million-year-old *yonka*. A Jamad Tengru does not lay bare the Sacred Things before the eyes of Outworlders. But my fingertips knew the curves of the old, worn iron hoops and the settings of the nine-sided thought crystals.

To think that I might wear it once again in the presence of the People . . . to hear the hill-shaking shout of the *haiyaa* . . . to lead again the war horde against the Hated Ones . . . and perhaps this time, to lead it to victory! If I said yes.

So I said yes.

While the Doctor settled his bill and checked out and Bolgov collected their luggage and got it into the freight shaft, the girl and I took the lift to the roof. Thank God for the age of automation: the lift was self-operationed and the only attendant on the parking roof was a camera eye. The girl blocked its view of me as we emerged into the open.

The sky was plum-purple by this time: dull, opaque, and dusty, like the bloom of a grape. We walked swiftly down the ranks of parked cars, not speaking to each other. The air was thick with the smell of sunbaked tar and lubricating oil, hot metal and rubber. Over all was the stink of Venice itself, a vast cacophony of stenches, wherein the odors of rotting garbage, stagnant water, and floating sewage dominated.

The first stars were out. They shone dully and looked neither convincing nor real. They were more like tarnished asterisks of foil pinned to the purple curtains of the crèche play or the dusty decorations on the domed ceiling of a run-down dance hall. Under this imitation sky we crossed the rooftop and found the Doctor's Lanzetti. Within a minute or two I was safely tucked away in the back seat, out of range of observation, with the rear windows opaqued. The luggage went thumping into the rear, and in a bit my companions climbed in, sealing the doors. The Doctor tuned in on Traffic Central, climbed steeply, and merged with the pattern. He chose a sideline which meandered across the country at five thousand feet in the general direction of Naples, but once the traffic had thinned out, he edged into a local level and unobtrusively followed a northerly route for a while, until he hit the turnoff for Strato 104. From then on we could relax, but he was careful to keep the car well within the speed and altitude limit. It would not have been wise to attract any attention from the traffic monitors, who spot-checked their radar from time to time.

We climbed at a leisurely rate until we were well over Europe. I switched on my seat scope and watched Switzerland go past beneath us and then Germany. You could see the lights of Munich and Frankfurt even from this height, but New Berlin was lost in a haze of pollution. Something very much like tears stung my eyes, and I glared them back stubbornly. This would probably be the last time in my life I would see the country of my birth. I had not gone home even in my years of wandering, for after my trial it had been subtly conveyed to me that Germany would not welcome me even as a tourist. I grinned wryly, remembering: a Berliner had held the coordinator's chair of the Associated Nations the year of my Martian crusade or rebellion or whatever it was. The fact that I, the archtraitor, shared the same homeland had been the ruin of his political ambitions—had, in fact, set his own party back to a very secondary place in the elections. My homeland nursed old grudges for a long time; if I had gone home, there would have been an unfortunate "accident."

The Doc chose the most commonly traveled tourist lane to the Moon but turned off into a side route a couple of hours later, as we neared our goal. I was dozing and missed it, but he followed the route around to the dark side, and very near the far terminator we decelerated with a bumb-bump that woke me. I shifted the seat scope to see the old Icarus, a black mass blotting out the stars, invisible except for its orbit lights. There was no mistaking the lumpy profile of an Icarus, with its control blister just forward of the center line, lending it a resemblance to a hunchbacked dolphin. We matched orbits; the cargo hold opened, and we berthed in the nearest of the twin cradles, broke seal when the doors were tight again, and climbed stiffly out.

The Doc was affability itself, now that a lot of the danger was over.

"Now, my young friend, we all have our several duties except for yourself, so permit me to escort you to your cabin and forgive me if I leave you there to your own devices. Have you dined?" I told him that I had not; I had not been aware of my emptiness until his remark reminded me. "Very well! You will find an autochef in your room and please make yourself at home. It will be some time before we break orbit—about an hour before Earthrise—so if you retire before then, please remember to strap yourself in your bunk. We will all have breakfast together in the morning, so until then . . ."

The cabin was smaller than was comfortable, but at least it had its own fresher cubicle, and the autochef produced a pretty good steak and surprised me with its Argentine coffee. I packed away my few effects in the wall cabinet, wondering what I was going to do for a change of clothes. But my host had anticipated this, and I found clean linen in my size and a couple of pairs of the zippered one-piece overalls spacemen call airsuit liners. I bathed, dined, and turned in, strapping the safety harness down, and turned off the lights. An hour before we edged around the Moon beyond the daylight terminator, I would be on my way to Mars.

It was hard for me to believe it was all coming true. I drifted into sleep, thinking about it, and my last coherent thought was a nagging twinge of guilt. For I knew that, despite what the Doctor thought, Ilionis was only a fairy tale. There was no lost Treasure City, and there was no lost treasure. This I knew beyond all doubt or question . . . I, who knew more of Mars and of its people than any other man of my world could ever know. This truth I could keep to myself for a while, but eventually it would come out, when we reached the site and found nothing there but eroded gullies full of gritty sand.

And when we got that far, I would be in very serious trouble.

3. Planetfall

There is no experience in life duller and more tedious than a space trip, particularly one of any real duration. By comparison, a strato flight from anywhere to anywhere is diverting, because at least you have clouds and a landscape below to look at; and an old-fashioned ocean voyage must have been heavenly, back in the days when they still used surface vessels.

But in space there simply is nothing at all to look at, which is why spacecraft are made without portholes or windows. Nothing lies beyond the hull fabric save dead black vacuum. There are lots of stars, but they all look alike and after your first glimpse of the "star-gemmed immensitudes" (as the poet calls them), you have seen everything there is. There is no variety in duplicating the experience.

The only parts of a space trip that afford the traveler anything at all in the way of scenic effects are departure and arrival. Generally, both are conducted in the vicinity of one moon or another, so you have the moonscape to look at and the more interesting planetscape beyond. But between the beginning and the end of your trip, there is nothing at all but dreary shipboard routine and absolute tedium. The drone and vibration of the drive itself are pleasurable in a way, but you only have them during acceleration and deceleration, and in between there is empty silence, punctuated by the whishing of the air ducts and the intermittent chime of the Meteor Proximity Alarm. God, you even begin to hunger for the minor excitement of the MPA after a while!

A Luna–Mars flight is tedium carried to the nth degree, especially when you make crossover in anything less luxurious than a Prometheus-class liner. The spacelines know how to cope with the boredom and provide everything from stereo views of Aristarchus at Earthrise, the Rings during a four-moon crossing, and other scenic spectaculars, to indoor sports, organized games, amateur theatricals, and a library of taped drama and variety shows.

Our four-man expedition, of course, had none of these diversions. We didn't even talk much among ourselves, although the Doctor made a heroic try at maintaining Old World geniality during dinner and strove to win a reputation as a brilliant conversationalist. The girl, Ilsa, had nothing to say to me, and as for my friend Konstantin, he had nothing to say to anybody.

But all spacecraft keep a library by Mandate law, if only to prevent people from going crazy during a long crossover. The *Antoine d'Eauville* had one that was quite decent, considering its quite natural preponderance of scholarly journals and texts (it was, after all, a museum boat). I got the impression that the craft was named after either the museum's founder or one of its more generous patrons, but no one ever enlightened me on the subject, so I never learned which.

I found enough to read to occupy most of my time, although outside of the voluminous scientific literature the general run of reading material was limited to turn-of-the-century European novelists and playwrights, with an unexpected sprinkling of midcentury writers from the South American states, mostly new to me. I had read no Borges at all since school and happening upon his inimitable genius was most enthralling. But the poets were almost entirely new discoveries. I had read, or looked into, a few of the Argentines—Ascasubi, Lugones, Almafuerte—but the others—such as a now-forgotten poet, once enormously popular, named Carriego—were all unknowns. Among them was Vázquez, the Nobel-prize winner, who became the most exciting of my new finds.

With nothing else to do in the endless monotony, I read virtually all day long. From time to time I would have to switch the machine off for no other reason than that it was overheating. Luckily, no one else aboard had my leisure, so I had the book tapes all to myself. The girl, I think, had a portable reader in her cabin; the Doctor was busy with a detailed redaction of the thought record; I don't know what Bolgov did—perhaps just sprawled on his bunk all day, glaring at the ceiling and sweating greasily—and the ship, of course, navigated itself.

In this strange way we traversed the distance between Luna and Mars, hardly seeing or speaking to each other except at meals. And I passed the monotony of transit gaining a modest education in obsolete European novelists and obscure South American poets. And without the least trouble or contact with a Mandate scout.

Mars became a big, mottled orange with spots of permafrost marking its poles. The Doctor expanded on his plans. It would have been begging for trouble, had he done the usual thing and moored the *d'Eauville* in a parking orbit and taken either the gig or the Lanzetti down. For surely the Earthside cops would have reconstructed what had happened and beamed an alert to their CA colleagues at Deimos Terminal. A quick scout would have spotted the *d'Eauville* without trouble and cut off the Doctor's escape route by simply sitting him out.

So he planned on something a trifle more risky, and that was to set the spacecraft down on the surface. Now an Icarus is about as small and light a craft as can safely be used for a crossover, but it's still cumbersome and tricky and fragile enough to make planetfall dangerous. The safety margin, however, got a boost from the fact that the gravity field of Mars is skimpy at best and the museum had already modified the *d'Eauville*'s design to take an outsized and high-powered drive engine for just such a purpose. Anyway, the Doctor was certain the computer could set her down on her tail in the flats west of the Drylands without blowing a venturi or springing a seam. I hoped he was right.

Once a safe planetfall was accomplished, the CA cops simply had no way of finding us, unless they had thirty times the manpower and flying strength they had had when I was last here. Because they could only locate the *d'Eauville* if they made an aerial search of the entire planetary surface, acre by acre. Which was a logistic impossibility.

The trouble with making planetfall in the westernmost Drylands was that we would have to do an awful lot of surface travel after landing. But that could not be helped: it would be like waving red flags and yelling "Look at me!" to go any closer to a major colony like Laestrygonum. And we needed a flat space with solid bedrock to set down on.

We didn't dare risk running so much as a single orbit, since we wanted to come down with the least possible chance of being sighted en route. In mid-crossover Bolgov had carefully programed the *d'Eauville*'s piloting and navigational computer to match intrinsics with the planet upon approach, so that the craft could segue smoothly from its original flightpath directly into a landing pattern without a break. It was a masterly job, and it went off without a hitch.

We came down in a slow glide, at an elongated angle to make maximum use of the thin atmosphere as a cushion to slow us down, since we didn't wish to run the risk of using the ordinary spiral braking orbit. A fast planetfall was of the essence, since every single second of time between the moment we broke out of deep space and the moment we hit topsoil we were in constant danger of being noticed on somebody's radar.

So we came in high up in the northern hemisphere over Arcadia and rode her down across Orcus at a shallow angle that tightened into a fish-hook arc. The glide path took us curving across the midregions of the Mare Sirenum in the direction of Aonius Sinus, with our terminus calculated just west of central Phaethontis.

The fabric began heating up till the hull would soon be a dull cherry-red. The Sirenum went hissing by beneath us in a rusty-purplish blur, much too hazy for us to make out anything but the largest craters. It was a shame we were going too fast to see the landscape, because this was very historic country. The area we were passing over had been the first chunk of local real estate that we Earthmen had ever gotten a close-up look at, even if it had only been a passing glance. I refer to the history-making Mariner IV fly-by, way back in 1965. The tiny, unmanned craft had skimmed across this same part of the Sirenum with all cameras whirring.

The only major canal that traverses the western half of Phaethontis is called the Thermodon. The Doc had hoped to be able to set the *d'Eauville* down near the west bank of the Thermodon, because the craft had been spray-enameled a dark mottled pattern and would blend with the colors of the canal, reducing the risk of a visual sighting. Coming out of our glide path for a taildown was a tricky bit of maneuvering, but the gyros were up to it, and we sat down, shaken by racking shudders that made the fabric screech and the structure groan. But we made it. The jets died with a cough, the craft trembled, then sat still. And then we all began to breathe again . . .

We had made it and in one piece.

"My compliments to the museum staff, Doc," I said in the unexpected silence. "Not many ships could live through a planetfall that tough."

"Thank you, my boy, but I believe the credit belongs to the Rolls-Royce people. They built good craft in those days . . ."

We unstrapped, levered ourselves out of the pressure chairs, which deflated with a piercing whistle, and began taking off our emergency suits and putting on the light-weight thermal suits we would need for Mars itself.

It seemed that only the Doctor and I had ever been on Mars before. So we helped the other two accustom themselves to the use of their respirators. Of the four of us, only I had ever undergone the Mishubi-Yakamoto treatments and could do without the artificial breathing boosters.

We had come down just where the Doc had planned. All about us, but tapering off due west, the canal extended like a four-foot-high miniature jungle. Seen from above— it was to be hoped!—the *Antoine d'Eauville* ought to blend unobtrusively with the shrubbery. Of course, to anyone crossing Phaethontis either afoot, on *slidar*, or by sand-tractor, it would stand out somewhat more prominently than a dozen sore thumbs, and that we could not help. However, this was the edge of the Drylands, and nobody ever comes this far south, not even the People, for the very good reason that there is nothing here to attract them.

Actors on the cube, stuck in a space-adventure epic, always make planetfall, crack the seal, and hit dirtside in no time flat. The conventions of stereovision drama aside, in

real life it takes from two to three hours before you are
ready to leave the spacecraft. You have to deprogram
your computer, dampen the power pile, let the fabric cool,
run triple checks for a burst seam, check out suits and respirators, and do a hundred other things. In our case, as we
would not be coming back to the craft until this whole expedition was over, it took closer to five hours before we
were ready to depart.

It was Bolgov's task to unlimber the gig. He sprung the
cargo port and lifted the gig out of its cradle next to the
Lanzetti, using the cargo crane, and set it down gently in
the dark mossy foliage.

The craft's gig, in this case, was an atmospheric skimmer instead of the usual two-man space boat. Actually,
they had chosen well in picking a skimmer, since it is the
fastest and most practical mode of transport that can be
used on Mars, certainly dozens of times faster and more
comfortable than a sand-tractor. Bolgov and Keresny then
began to stow our gear aboard the skimmer. I suppose I
should have gone to lend them a hand, but I could not do
it, somehow. I wanted to savor to the fullest my first moment on Mars after all these lonely, empty, bitter years.

So I came out of the airlock below the control blister,
climbed down the extensible ladder, jumped down to the
springy moss, and then just stood there for a long moment,
tasting the dry, spicy tang of the cold, thin air of Mars,
feeling the crispness of the rubbery-tendriled moss underfoot, and the exhilarating lightness of Martian gravity.
How long, how long since I had tasted that ozonous tang
at the back of my mouth, how long since I had felt the
skin of my face pucker and roughen to the biting chill in
the air . . . ?

I stood there silent and motionless for a long time,
brooding on old, glorious dreams and the memory of
comrades I had known and loved, all dead men now, with
six feet of dry Martian dust their everlasting home. My
eyes filled and ran over with tears. Tears that vanished
and were gone almost in the same instant they were shed.
Tears that the desiccated Martian air drank thirstily,
grateful for the rare gift of moisture . . .

I looked about me, eyes blurring, remembering . . .

My memory drifted back to my first landing on Mars, years and years ago. When I was young and raw and green and idealistic. I recalled how we had ridden down in a little, crowded, rattletrap satellite shuttle from Deimos Terminal, flying east across the Tharsis region to make planetfall at the debarkation camp out in Isidis Regio. I remembered how I had felt then when I first came out of the lock with the other new arrivals, breathing hoarsely through the strange, ill-fitting respirators, waiting to pile on the long tractor train for an interminable, bumpy ride across the craterlets to Syrtis. Staring about me then, I had been struck dumb with awe at the utter strangeness of the scene—the dim, flat stretch of the Isidis dustlands; the grim, dark, shaggy bulk of Syrtis Major, thrusting like a wedge-shaped peninsula deep into the sea of fantastic yellow sands; and the glistening pile that was Syrtis Colony itself, rising on the oddly near horizon, a haze of dim foggy blue from the earth-density air trapped within its hemispherical MPB field.

As we had approached the colony itself, several of my fellow travelers were loudly exclaiming that they had thought the city was supposed to be *domed*. Did Colonial Administration expect them to wear these uncomfortable masks *all* the time?

I remember the offhand manner in which the tractor jockey, an old Mars hand, lean as a rail and mahogany brown from deep space radiation, explained laconically that the original colony had been set up under a collapsible plastic dome—"too damned easily collapsible," was his joke. But that was back before they invented the molecular-potential barrier field, an energy plane whose surface-tension charge repelled air molecules and stabilized internal air pressure, which made it possible to build up and maintain an atmospheric pressure of Earth-norm density—

"*Oh!*"

The mood snapped at the unexpected sound. I turned. The girl, Ilsa, had followed me out of the lock and was taking her first look at the surface of Mars. I went over and stood beside her; her eyes were wide with amazement, and she sucked in her breath in a gasp and sank her fingers in my arm. I didn't blame her: your first actual look at the Martian landscape can be an amazing experience.

The craters are the first surprise Mars has for you. There are so many of them, and they are everywhere. Some of them are just little pockmarks in the ground that you can barely put your fist into; and they range all the way up to the super-monster, in the southeastern corner of whose ringwall the *entire colony* of Sun Lake City is built.

Her fingers dug in. I glanced down, seeing her wide-eyed stare beneath the goggles, and grinned faintly, remembering my own astonishment. For the second big surprise is when you discover that the Red Planet is not red at all, but a patchwork crazy-quilt of yellow dustlands and blue moss growth, broken here and there by vivid patches of raw orange and brilliant, impossible purple.

The first settlers couldn't get over their amazement at the color scheme. Which is absurd, but human enough. In hindsight it's hard to understand how anybody ever made the mistake of thinking Mars was going to be red. After all, one of the Russian scientists, Tikhov or somebody like that, deduced that Martian vegetation, if there turned out to actually *be* any Martian vegetation, would have to be blue in order for the planet to look red from the viewpoint of Earthside visual astronomers. He realized that more than a century and a half ago, back around 1909. And it wasn't even that clever a deduction in the first place. All it took was a fair grasp of the mechanics of light, which the old-time boys had figured out even earlier, starting with Newton.

We just stood there for a while, just staring around. The sky was dead, dull black, lightening a little toward dusty violet at the edges of the horizon where the air molecules got a chance to bunch up a bit and do some diffracting. The stars were piercingly sharp and clear, and they were weirdly different from the stars you see at night, Earthside. These did not twinkle, did not waver in the slightest, and they were the damndest colors. Earthside the stars mostly seem glittering, flashing white, sometimes with a touch of blue or red, but that is simply because the faint colors of starlight have little chance of getting through Earth's mulligan stew of an atmosphere. Here they blaze in the rarest of colors: half a dozen shades of green and blue, all tones from pale yellow through red, and even a few you simply wouldn't believe, like Alpha Derceto, which is pure brown, and Delta Erigius, which is puce.

She was looking up, searching about. Grinning, I asked her if she was looking for the moons, and she nodded and asked where they were. I tried to tell her that they were simply too damn small to be visible to the unaided vision, except under certain rather rare circumstances, but she found that impossible to believe.

"But that's simply insane!" she said, the thin air making her voice tinny and flat. "Why, back home you can even see a communications satellite on clear nights, if you know where to look. And they're only ten or fifteen feet across, where here— Well, Deimos, the nearest moon, is supposed to have a diameter of ten miles. It's just crazy to say you simply can't see them at all!"

"I didn't say you couldn't see them at all, I said they were too small to be seen except under certain rare conditions," I reminded her. "One of those conditions is knowing just where to look. In the first place, Deimos is the *outer* moon, not the nearest, and it's the only one you can see without magnification, because it moves so very slowly —it takes two days, local time, to cross the sky. The trouble is that it has a lousy albedo, and it's too high for its size to make any difference in its degree of visibility."

She sounded dubious. "Is that really true? What about the other one?"

"Phobos you never can see at all," I told her, "even though it's bigger than Deimos, has a higher albedo—that means 'reflecting power,' by the way. It's also very, very, *very* close to the surface of the planet."

"Then why can't you see it?"

"Because it moves too fast. It goes all around the planet three whole times in a single day, and if you don't think that is *fast,* well, stop and think about it."

"But I still don't see—!"

"You simply can't know where precisely to look for it. It's a question of albedo, for the most part. You see, Mars is so much farther from the sun than Earth is that we don't get more than a tiny fraction of the light Earth gets. Now back on Earth, a full moon is dazzlingly bright, because it has an awful lot of light to reflect. But here the moons have only a tiny fraction of that much light, and they have lower albedos too.

"But the main problem with Phobos is not that it is much too dim and dark to show up very well, but it whizzes by so rapidly that you never know just where in the sky to look for it at any given time. You have to search the sky from horizon to horizon, slowly and carefully, and even then, under the best of conditions you'd have to be mighty lucky to—"

I broke off as moss rustled and squeaked under heavy boots behind me.

"Your first lesson in Marsology, my dear?" Dr. Keresny broke in amiably. "Forgive me for interrupting, but the skimmer is all packed. Cn. Tengren, we are ready when you are."

4. Beyond Death River

The skimmer was cramped, crowded, and hot. Leastways, it seemed hot to me, for my surgically implanted energy centers were already beginning to adjust to the freezing temperatures. My companions, on the other hand, were shivering even in their thermal suits and were happy to warm up; happy, also, to remove their bulky respirators for a while.

Our arrival time had been calculated to a nicety. The sun—which looked shockingly pale and shrunken and cool from here—was at its zenith. That gave us several hours of flying time till nightfall. Once darkness came down, of course, it would be impossible to keep on flying, and we would have to camp for the night. But by then we would be deep in the Drylands, with lots of real estate behind us and our journey well begun.

With Bolgov handling the controls, we flew due west. The shaggy border of the canal shrank behind us, merging in a purplish-brown line that seemed to stretch across the world from north to south with such perfect precision that you could swear it had been inked across the dustlands with a mapping pen. The canals of Mars are really patchy, broken areas of low, thick-leafed shrubs and very dense moss which flourish—if that's really the word for such marginal survival—along subsurface crustal lesions where moisture has been trapped for ages by sheets of solid bedrock. From a distance, due to optical effects, these fertile stretches of vegetation seem to take on an astoundingly regularity which suggested to early astronomers that they were vast artificial waterways, like those our own ancestors built at Suez and Panama. The optical illusion is a simple one, really: look at any photograph in a newsfax. Seen way up close, the picture breaks down into a pattern of square dots, but held at arm's length the dots merge and blur into tones between gray and black.

The skimmer droned on across the dustlands of western Phaethontis at the low altitude old Mars hands call dune-hopping. Bolgov might be surly and heavy handed, but he knew his trade. There's quite a trick to keeping a skimmer aloft, even with all the help of the enormous, paper-thin extensible foils.

Ahead of us, and a trifle to the north, the hilly edges of the Cimmerium drifted closer. A dark, dull, fairly even, plateaulike mass of brownish-purple, slashed by the unbroken ink black of the great ravines which cleft it asunder in a thousand places. An area like the Mare Cimmerium is an amusing contradiction in terms. Early astronomers, noting the large, dark-colored areas that mottled the surface of Mars, thought they were seas and named them thus in Latin. The element of contradiction comes in later. That is, when the first expeditions got here, they discovered the larger, lighter-colored areas, the dust-lands, were what had been left behind when the real seas evaporated millions of years ago, and the dark patches were actually former continents, cracked apart by gullies the size of the Grand Canyon by the shrinking of the crust.

I began idly questioning Keresny as to the site of the so-called Treasure City. The ancient thought record he had found up at Thoth-Nepenthes had given the site with particular detail. Scholars have spent twenty years striving to figure out the peculiar geographical notation employed by the Ancients and have come up with a rough but workable system. The location revealed in the thought record worked out to south latitude 27' 11°, east longitude 140' 37°. That would place the city very deep in the Mare Cimmerium, about equidistant between the two dustlands of Hesperia and Eridania. And that meant we had a lot of scenery to cover before we could even get close to the goal of our quest.

"Well, the best way to do it is to circle south of the Cimmerium, keeping well out in the dustlands," I advised. "Flying over the Cimmerium plateau itself is very tricky business, and skimmers don't handle very easily at any kind of altitude."

"That's going to take forever," Bolgov growled over his shoulder. "We're too far south as it is, right now."

"It's going to be quite a trip," I admitted. "But an old plateau like the Cimmerium is dangerous. Riddled with fumaroles that create sharp updrafts that could shatter your foils, knock you out of the air. Down below most of the Maria are pockets of natural gas that leak steadily into the atmosphere under terrific pressure. You don't have to cope with anything like that over the lower dustlands."

"What happens, then, when we arrive at our longitude?" the Doctor asked. "How can we go north into Mare Cimmerium, unless we use the skimmer?"

I shrugged. "We'll have to leave the skimmer as close to the foot of the plateau as we can get and go ahead on foot. With any kind of luck we might be able to find a hefty ravine that cuts deeply into the plateau on the north–south line. Some of them are as big as the Grand Canyon of Wyoming; some are even bigger."

"Do you suppose we could fly up the ravine?" Ilsa asked. "If they're *that* big . . . I mean, the Grand Canyon is several miles wide at some points, isn't it? Surely, despite our wingspread, we could navigate without fouling them."

I shook my head. "No, you see, it isn't a matter of fouling the wings—the foils, I mean—some of the chasms are twenty miles wide from cliff wall to cliff wall. But the bottom of the ravines are pimpled with fumaroles, and the gas escapes in narrow jets under tremendous pressure. The ravines are more dangerous to a skimmer than the plateau itself, for that reason. No, we'll just have to go it on foot. Unless we happen to run into some of the People and can get *slidars* from them. But that's unlikely, way down here near the South Pole cap."

Brother Konstantin grumbled a bit and swore about dragging out the time factor, but the Doctor put his foot down, saying that here I was the expert and that my advice was sound and we would follow it. After that the conversation lapsed lamely into silence. I leaned back against the luggage net and dozed off.

We flew on until sundown. The atmosphere of Mars is too thin to make for gorgeous sunsets—too thin too for light to linger in long twilights. On Mars, darkness falls suddenly with sunset, all at once: like a great black curtain drawn swiftly across the heavens.

Bolgov brought the skimmer down to a long, easy, gliding stop, talcum-fine sand dust hissing under the runners. By the glow of a Bronston lamp we set up the vacuum-tight thermal tents, while Ilsa prepared food. It was very hard to set a fire in this oxygen-starved atmosphere, but Keresny was an old Mars hand and knew that already. So the provisions included some self-heating containers the Mandate cops use during field problems: you twist the top to break the seal, wait five minutes, then spoon out the hot stew or soup or whatever. I wanted to eat out under the stars, but as my companions would find it rather hard to eat dinner through a respirator, we ate in the larger tent that the Doctor would share with his granddaughter. Keresny had brought along a canister of champagne, and we drank a toast to the success of our search, but the change in atmospheric pressure made the champagne flat, and it tasted stale.

That night I dreamed of Yakla, the little silver beads glittering like stars in the night-black curtain of her hair. It was not a happy dream, and I woke before dawn as weary as if I had not slept at all.

We flew on all that day and all of the next crossing the broad isthmus of the Simois into the upper tip of Electris. By the next day we had flown across the Scamander canal and were in the dustlands of Eridania. It took us a whole day of steady travel to cross the broad bowl of yellow dust, and we were all restless and quarrelsome from being cooped up for so many endless hours in the narrow confines of the skimmer's cabin. Bolgov was grumbling over the fact that we could have set the *d'Eauville* down in the Scamander instead of the Thermodon and saved ourselves two days of flying. Keresny, with his saintly patience wearing a bit thin, told once again of the dangers of trying for a planetfall so hazardously near to Laestrygonum colony, which was on the Sinus just north of the Cimmerium.

The next day we flew north by northwest over a broad mossy zone crisscrossed by the darker belts of two minor canals, into the southern tip of Hesperia. And by sundown we were nearly as far as we could get by flying. The next morning we flew due north, feeling our way across the patchy moss-lands, the shaggy, chasm-riven bulk of the Mare looming ever nearer. With great caution we skirted the south base, looking for a ravine that ran due north. The Doctor had a big CA survey map open across his knees and studied it carefully.

"Hareton Rill looks like our best bet," he said. "We should reach its mouth in approximately ten minutes. It will take us inland about forty kilometers without causing us to diverge much from our course, but then we will have to ascend to the roof of the plateau. Lucky that I thought to carry plenty of line and climbing gear."

"Lucky too that the Martian gravity is so light," I said. "It will make it easier to ascend the rock face."

He beamed at the girl. "It was Ilsa's notion that we might need it, although I suspect she was thinking of utilizing the gear to descend into a treasure vault or cavern, rather than using it to climb a cliff."

We went on for a bit, found the mouth of the Rill, and nosed in very cautiously. The floor was a jumble of broken stone blocks the size of three-story houses, and there was no place visible within sight where it would be safe to set the skimmer down, so Bolgov brought her around in a fairly tight circle and headed out again into the open dustlands of Hesperia, circled, and took her taxiing down. He taxied on hissing runners to the mouth and brought her to a dead stop.

We wrestled the skimmer into the mouth of the Rill and found a safe nook to store her away under a bit of camouflage netting, where she would be unlikely to be discovered by chance. Carrying the little craft across the powdery sands would have been one hell of a job back on Earth; here, of course, the gravity was only about four-tenths as strong, and it was not as tough as it might seem.

This done, we loaded our backpacks on the lightweight, collapsible aluminum sledge, and trudged into the Rill on foot, Bolgov taking the first turn dragging the sledge.

The ground was very uneven and knee deep in places with heaped rubble, fine in texture, like crushed gravel. This was the result of erosion from the rock face. Not erosion due to wind and water, of course, but the aeon-slow action of day and night, of frigid night and comparatively warmer day. The endless centuries of slight expansion and contraction, working away on the rock, cracked off pebbles over the ages. This was hard stuff to walk through, and it made the going difficult.

The sledge itself was difficult to drag, although it was certainly light enough. Bolgov cursed sulfurously, trying to jam the ungainly thing through the narrow interstices between the colossal boulders. The job would have been much easier if the sledge had been equipped with wheels, but this was a dustlands sledge, with ski runners. Still, it was a lot easier than lugging all the gear on our backs.

It was pretty rugged going. Respirators are useful, well-designed gadgets, but they cannot cope with outdoor labor very well. We needed frequent rest stops, and we all took a turn at dragging the sledge, even the old man.

The deeper we got into the Rill, the more the darkness closed around us. The cliffwalls were about seven miles apart at the mouth, but they soon came together, narrowing to shut away most of the sky. We began to pass some of the fumaroles I had mentioned earlier. The first one was just a pocketlike depression in the ground with a black, irregular hole at the bottom of it, and a steamy vapor ascending in a vague wisp. It did not look very dangerous, I must admit. Bolgov eyed it and made a sour grunt. He fixed me with a surly eye.

"This kind of stuff is going to knock down a *skimmer?*" he demanded. "Kack on that. My grandmother's samovar kicked up a hell of a lot more fuss than that pothole and gave off more steam too!"

"From the greenish hue of the escaping gases, that looks like methane, not steam," the Doctor said genially. "Still, I must admit Konstantin is right. It does not look very dangerous." He glanced at me dubiously. I shrugged.

It was about time for another rest stop, so I suggested we halt right here. A few minutes later the fumarole exploded in a ground-shaking spray of solid green-yellow vapor that shot a half-mile in the air in an almost-solid steam, like the jet from a fire hose. As I had suspected, the gas geyser was a periodic.

"See?" I grinned. Bolgov paled, under the coating of fine dust that masked his swarthy face, and Ilsa bit her lip. A jet that strong would rip the wing off an atmospheric liner or punch a hole through the fuselage of a helicopter. Any flimsy little skimmer that got hit with the full force of that geyser would come down over half an acre in pieces the size of your toenail clippings.

We went forward in silence.

I had made my point.

After a day of trudging around, between, and some-times across boulders as big as houses, we were weary in every muscle. We slept soundly that night and woke to find the thermal tents covered with hoarfrost from the moisture our circulator valves had leaked during the night. We were stiff and sore and very much in want of a bath and a shave, but those were Colony luxuries; here we must go dirty and unshaven, nursing our water supplies. When those ran low we would have to use the recycling system, but perhaps we could reach our destination before we had to drink purified waste fluids.

I had done it many times, back in the wild years, but it was nothing to look forward to.

We trudged on, and the Rill flattened out a bit, making the going a bit easier.

By early afternoon we reached Death River. I dropped the loops of the sledge from my arms, and we stood to-gether on the brink looking down at the thing.

Next to me Ilsa shivered suddenly.

"What *is* it?" she whispered.

"I suppose it has to be one of the natural wonders of Mars," I said grimly. "But it's a damned unpleasant one. Still, it's a mystery. No one's ever found another. Not that anyone is anxious to."

The People call it *Farad-i-Janhg,* River of Death.

It's a deep, narrow, rocky gorge that falls to a narrow bottom. The name *river* suggests running water, but run-ning water is about the rarest thing on all of the planet. This river is a river of gases. Gases that are deadly poison to breathe. A weird, flowing stream of heavier-than-air va-pors that drift sluggishly along the bottom of the steep-sid-ed gorge. An eerie sight, surely. And a deadly hazard, im-possible to wade through, even with respirators.

The presence of the famous Death River is why this particular Rill out of tens of thousands happens to have a name on the map. Hareton discovered it at the end of his Hesperian expedition of '52.

He went down on a line to take a sample.

Then he tried to cross it, using a respirator and a thermal suit.

He's still down there, somewhere.

"So how the hell do we get across?" the Ukrainian growled.

Keresny began unpacking one of the bundles and took out a grapnel gun. He inserted a compressed-air canister and after three or four tries managed to sink the grapnel in the far bank of the river. Then we made the muzzle end of the line secure around a big hunk of rock and tested the line for tension.

We were going to have to go across, hand over hand, at least the first of us.

I volunteered for that job. I pulled on the heavy fiberglass gloves, got a good hold on the line and slid over the edge. My feet were swinging free about nine or ten feet meters above the upper layer of poisonous mist. But it wasn't the gas that scared me; if I fell, I'd die of a broken neck before the gas could bother me. Because the floor of Death River is solid rock, and it's a long way down.

Carefully, I began to swing hand over hand the length of the line. The heavy gloves kept the wire from cutting into my hands, and the weak gravity field made me only four-tenths my usual hundred and ninety pounds. But it was not a comfortable trip. And I kept thinking about that grapnel and wondering how securely the airgun had shot its prongs into the ancient, soft, crumbling rock.

Once across, I swung my legs up and elbowed myself prone on the bank.

It wasn't a thing I'd like to do every day.

The girl came next. Since the south bank of the gorge was a little higher than the bank where I stood, the Doctor had thought she could cross more easily using a roller. This was a little hand bar with hollow-rimmed wheels which rode the line. They helped her over the edge, and she kicked off gamely and came flying across the gorge, hair streaming loosely.

I watched the grapnel with steady eyes, ready to grab for it at the first sign her weight was beginning to pry the prongs loose.

Her face was pale, and her little jaw was set grimly, and she had forgotten to breathe, but she was game and flew across the River of Death without the fainting fits or hysterics most Earthside girls might be expected to have.

As the north wall of the gorge swung up toward her, she kicked out against it with booted feet, braking the slide. Then I reached down over the edge, got one arm around her small waist, and hoisted her up to solid ground.

She was a light little thing, like a child; and she fitted snugly into the curve of my shoulder.

As I boosted her onto her feet, a lock of her straw-colored hair whipped silkenly against my cheek. I drew in a breath of warm fragrance, the odor of her hair.

Then she snatched herself away from me, eyes blazing with a cold fury. "I don't like being touched—by a thing like you!" she hissed.

I said nothing as she spun on her heel, turning away from me. What was there I could say?

We got the others across safely too. The Doctor came next, and he used the hand roller, which I slid back along the line to him. Getting the sledge across was going to be an impossible job, so he left it where it was. Bolgov lashed each of the packs to the roller and slid them across to us, one by one.

Then it was his turn. Scorning the roller, he swung across hand over hand, as I had done. He crossed slowly, huffing and blowing, face purple, beefy body swaying like an ungainly pendulum, kicking out with his heavy boots for extra momentum. Wheezing and panting from the exertion, he scrambled up and sat down on the ledge by us, flexing his tired hands.

Then we knocked off and had some lunch.

Then Ilsa screamed!

She had gone on further up the Rill, exploring a bit while we got the packs across. She had gone around a bend between two huge, hill-sized boulders.

The scream was flat and devoid of echoes in the thin air. I jumped to my feet, heart trip-hammering in the cage of my ribs, and went after her, boots thudding against loose rock, raising swift-settling clouds of canary-yellow dust.

I rounded the bend and came to a halt beside her.

She was standing all stiff, hands clasped at her chin. I saw at once the thing that had startled her. It would startle most people.

A dead man hung head down on a beam of wood.

He was very, very dead and had hung there for a very long time, years maybe—from the condition he was in it was hard to tell. A crudely hammered copper nail had been driven through his crossed feet at the ankles. That was all; no other wounds on the body. They had nailed · him to the beam and left him there to die slowly.

The dry Martian air had sucked every drop of moisture from his naked body, leaving it shrunken and lean and leathery as a mummy. Behind me Bolgov was swearing in a shaking voice in Russian. At my shoulder the Doctor was breathing lightly and rapidly in little short gusts, like a bird.

"What is it?" the girl whimpered.

"It . . . seems to be a crucifixion, my dear."

"It's a marker," I said. "We must be getting into clan territory." I pointed at the old flakes of weathered blue paint on the bony breast of the shrunken thing. "That is the marker of the Moon Dragon nation. The dead man is a sort of no-trespassing sign."

We shivered, although it was no colder than usual.

As a warning sign it was very effective.

We went back to where we had left the packs and rested for a time and had lunch. Then we pushed off, circling around the wooden beam and its grisly burden and went up the Rill until the world darkened with the coming of night.

5. Into the Sea of Darkness

This part of Mars, the Mare Cimmerium, the Sea of Darkness as the old Earthside astronomers called it, is one of the wildest, most rugged, least known, and most dangerous portions of the planet.

That warning sign was a bordermark.

The crucified man had been a member of some rival or stranger clan.

He had trespassed on the borders of the Moon Dragon nation, and they had killed him for it.

We were trespassing too.

It was something to think about . . .

The People call this plateau Chun. The Riders of Chun are fierce warriors, deadly foes, firm friends. The Low Clans hail me as Jamad Tengru; they are vowed to serve my will. But what about the High Clans, like the Riders of Chun, the warriors who fight under the Moon Dragon banner? Would they recognize the Iron Crown? Would they respect the vow?

Something else to think about.

That night I couldn't get to sleep, so after a while I gave it up, got into my thermal suit and boots, unsealed the tent flap, and went out under the cold ferocity of the stars to think.

Ilsa was there, leaning against a rock, her yellow hair a pale flame in the star glow.

I would have gone silently back to my tent and let her be, but she heard the crunch and squeak of boot heels in the powdery sand and turned and saw me. So I went up to her.

"Can't sleep?"

She shook her head.

"Take a pill; sometimes slogging by foot makes you so tired, even in this light gravity, that you can't sleep without one. Our bodies were not designed for this world . . ."

"It's not that," she said a bit stiffly. "It's just that I'm dying for a smoke."

I laughed. "Well, you'll get over that; you'll have to, I'm afraid. Can't smoke wearing a respirator and can't live without one, either. So you'll have to learn to live without aromatiques!"

Her face was a cool mask in the starry brilliance. She was so beautiful the sight of her made my throat go dry. I had not felt this way toward any woman since Yakla . . . died.

She said nothing.

"Sure it's just that you need an aromatique? Or is it something else?"

She shrugged dispiritedly. "It's this whole messy business, I guess," she said. "I don't know what to do. Grandfather has always been a decent, honorable man. And now he's trying to steal treasure from people who never harmed him . . . breaking laws. It's—it's just not *like* him!"

I nodded somberly. "Gold fever, they call it. It can hit anybody."

"But he's never been an—an adventurer! He's a scientist, a scholar; a respected man in his field, with a reputation. I have the most awful feeling that we're going into bad trouble . . . and I don't know anything I can do to stop it from happening."

"Why did you come along if you feel like this? You could have stayed back home in Switzerland or wherever your home is."

"I went to school in Switzerland. Our home is in Paris, or near there, in a little village up the Seine. We've been living there quietly ever since grandfather retired from the museum and left the Moon; I've been taking care of him. He's all the family I've got now. Somehow it just didn't seem right that I should let him go off on this crazy treasure hunt without me."

"Well, I don't much like the idea of the treasure hunt

either, but I think it will all come out in the end. Your grandfather may not get any treasure, but I don't think he will lose anything more precious than a dream," I said. "I think I can understand what happened to him. An old man's dreams . . ."

She turned to look at me.

"What do you mean?"

I spread my hands. "Scientists are dedicated men, sure; but they're human enough, God knows. There's a spark of ego way down deep under all that selfless dedication. There's not a man of them that doesn't hanker to be remembered as another Pasteur or Einstein. Your grandfather finished a lifetime devoted to his work and found himself with nothing to show for it—nothing but a 'reputation.' That's small change, for a man who hoped to be one of the immortals of science. Reputations are a ten-for-a-penny these days."

She turned on me like a cat.

"You should know all about that—yours is rather unsavory," she flashed. "It is sickening to hear a cheap traitor like you defaming an old man who worked all his life for science! He may have come out of it all with nothing much to show for all those years of hard work—but at least he still has his patriotism!"

My face was stiff, and my mouth felt wooden, but worse words than those have been flung in my teeth before this, and I have become accustomed to the taste of them.

I let the silence stretch between us for a time. Then I said, softly: "Is that what's been between us all this time —the word *traitor?* Because something's been wrong. You've disliked me from the moment we met. From *before* we met. Is that what it is?"

After a while she said yes in a small voice.

I thought it over for a little. Then: "I'm not going to try to defend my actions to you, but not because they don't maybe need defending. Because I don't think you are the proper person to judge them."

She started to say something, but I overrode her and went on.

"Listen to me. There are two kinds of traitors. The first

is the man who betrays a name, a word, a bit of cloth, a colored place on a map. The second is the man who betrays his own instinct; who goes against what his heart and reason tells him is the truth. I am the first. I will *not* be the second.

"Listen! When I came here ten years ago to work for the Colonial Administration, I was just as young and good and patriotic as you. They put me in the Office of Native Affairs, and most of my work was out among the People, as the Martian natives call themselves. I had all your own fine ideals. I loved home and flag and mother. But when I got out here and saw the things that were being done under that same flag, I wanted to tear it down and dirty it. I wanted to raise my voice in a yell so loud that every single human soul back Earthside could hear me. I wanted to tell them the things I had seen out here. I wanted my voice to reach into the council chambers of the fine and glorious world state you love so much and tell them the horrors that our own people were wreaking out here in the high, holy name of that world state."

I had forgotten to keep calm. My face was hot, and my voice was bitter and loud. But to hell with keeping calm.

"I saw a proud, poor, ancient culture being ripped apart. I watched a magnificent civilization being looted with all the expertise of modern technology. Tombs and temples—shrines that had been holy places before we crawled out from under the last ice age—being knocked apart by bulldozers to get at the gold that might or might not be there. Oh, Christ, the Conquistadors who gutted the Aztecs and the Incas should have had bulldozers! And flame guns too: you should watch a couple dozen Colonial guards tie an old priest up and burn his legs off with a flame gun to get him to tell them where gold is hidden. And then rape his daughter in front of his eyes—one grinning Earthman after another—until she dies of it—*and even after*—making him watch it, all the while, until he is dead too. Oh, yes, even a Swiss finishing school education can't help you against a sight like that! You forget all about loving home and flag and mother, and you forget about our sacrosanct and perfect world state after a few sights like that one."

"I don't believe——"

"Shut up until I've finished. Do you know what a *huakan* is?"

"Those godstones . . . ?"

"They aren't godstones, they're ancestral tablets, memorials, sort of like gravestones. Beautiful tablets of yellow Martian jade, covered with incised hieroglyphics no one alive can read anymore. Each 'family' has one; some are a million years old. The luck of a family lives in its *huakan*; the deeds and names of every ancestor are carved there. The People venerate them, like Chinese ancestor worship, but without the element of superstition." I drew a deep breath and went on in a ragged-edged voice. "One day I saw two happy neo-Catholic missionaries waddling home from a *huakan* ground. They had been about the Lord's business and were swapping a bottle of brandy back and forth. They had been busy driving the devil from Mars, you see, and helping to convert the natives from their lamentable paganism. I went into the *huakan* ground and looked around. Those two priests had borrowed a maul and smashed thirty or forty tablets to rubbish. Smashed them into gravel, understand? Irreplaceable tablets that had stood untouched for thousands of years . . . tablets the worst criminal outcast among the People would rather die than desecrate . . . laughing, swigging down brandy, taking turns, those happy priests had trampled them into wreckage, because they thought they were *idols*." My face felt hard and cold as a mask of bronze. I couldn't see the girl very well because my eyes were full of stinging tears. "One of those bastards is a bishop right now," I said.

The girl was crying, frightened. But I went on brutally, saying the things that needed saying.

"Do you know how the Colonial Administration *really* works? Do you know that one Administrator General went home a rich man because he hooked enough natives on heroin—*at gunpoint*—and made several fortunes having the junk smuggled to Mars on Mandate cruisers and selling it to the poor bastards for gems, furs, and bullion——

the price of a fix? Because once hooked on the junk, they would die without it? And the son of a bitch who followed him into office went home wealthy too. All he did was buy two fat Wetlands plantations and stock them with cheap labor. Slave labor. Natives forced into slave chains, also at gunpoint. With the starry flag of the Associated Nations waving overhead."

My voice was hoarse and raw now. "I didn't become a traitor to my own people because I wanted to, but because I *had* to. Because my people stopped being my people and became my enemies. Because by that time I had fallen in love with this poor, worn-out old corpse of a planet and in love with the pitiful remnants of its once-mighty people. They became . . . *my* people. And their cause became mine. And their enemies became my enemies."

"And now you're as bad as we are!" she cried. "If all this is—is true—why are you helping to loot Ilionis of its treasure? You're gold mad too, like—like grandfather!"

"Number one, there is no Lost City and no treasure, as the old man is going to find out when we get there," I snarled. "And number two, I would sell my soul for a ticket here. And maybe I have . . ."

She looked at me in bewilderment.

"What do you mean? No Lost City—no treasure? But grandfather's thought record . . . he's convinced it can't be a forgery!"

"And he's right, it can't. But it can be a lie or a legend. A document may be authentic as all hell, but that's no proof that what's written on it is truth. I know the People better than any Earthman ever has. I know the People, and I know their ways. Their sagas and stories. They lost the bright, splendid civilization they once had when this dustball of a world was fresh and young and new, when it had a rich atmosphere and rolling seas. They like to pretend to themselves that not all of that vanished greatness has departed; that somewhere a bit of it lingers on, like the last remnant of the Golden Age."

"You mean . . . it's just a fable? You *know* it's just a fable, and you let grandfather go on believing it? You kept your mouth shut and let him live in his dream and break all those laws for nothing . . . *just so you could take advantage of his delusion?"*

I said simply: "Would he have believed me if I had told him it was just a golden dream? No. He wants that dream, and he will cling to it at any cost, against any proof to the contrary. And if he is crazy enough to come here in pursuit of it . . . Well, I'd have to be crazy too, not to take advantage of his offer."

And it was just then that a harsh voice rang out, right behind me.

"Is this dirty Cat-lover messing with you, miss?"

I started to turn, but before I could, a fist the size of a boiled ham caught me right behind the ear. I went down on my knees hard, slamming against the gritty dust, while the world swung around me in dizzy, whirling fashion. Then I took a boot in the ribs that came out of nowhere and knocked me over on my side; and the world got very dark for a while.

Then the smell of warm yellow hair was heady in my nostrils, and I pried bleary eyes open to see the girl's face bending over me, white and scared in the starlight. Somewhere off to the side Bolgov was swearing viciously. I got my head up off the girl's lap and climbed to my feet unsteadily.

The Doctor was there, his fine old face strained and serious and a small energy gun clenched in his long fingers. The business end of the gun was trained on Bolgov's guts. The big man stood straddle legged, his face flushed and angry, nursing bloody knuckles. I couldn't tell whether it was my blood on his hand or his own.

"Are you all right, Cn. Tengren?" the old man called in a voice that quavered a little. However unsteady his voice, the hand that held the gun did not waver a millimeter.

"I'm in one piece, thanks."

Then I went over to where Bolgov stood. I reached out and took his throat in my hand in an old *Akita* grip. He gaped like a fish and went down to his knees in front of me; it was either that or have his throat ripped out. Keresny cried out something sharply, but I was not listening.

Bolgov gagged and gawked and fumbled at my fingers.

"Put your hands down at your sides or I'll ruin you," I said in a level voice, spacing the words. He did so. Then I leaned down and looked him straight in the eyes. They were wide and full of fear, those eyes, and the whites were sallow and blood-shot, and they were weeping tears of astonishment and pain.

"Cat-lover," I said. "This is the second time you've used that word on me. The first time I almost broke your jaw. This time I am not going to do anything. But listen to me, Brother Konstantin: if you ever call me by that name again, I'll break you in half. Believe me."

I let go of him, and he sprawled, gagging and spitting in the dirt. I turned on my heel, went past the white-faced girl, ignored the appeal in her wide blue eyes, and went back to my tent.

It had been a hard day and a busy night.

I slept like a babe.

All the next day, as we went on, my eyes kept roaming to the top of the cliffs. The Rill was narrowing, and it was a perfect trap. And they were out there somewhere, that I knew. The Riders of Chun; waiting.

It was only a matter of time.

By mutual consent we hardly spoke to one another all day. Bolgov did not speak to me, did not even look at me, at least not while I was facing him. But often, when my back was turned, I could feel his hard, ugly eyes boring into the back of my neck, hating me. I could almost feel the itch in his stubby fingers, yearning for the butt of his gun.

The Doctor had little to say, sunk deep in his own thoughts. Had Ilsa passed on to him my true opinion of this crazy quest for a lost city that was never there in the first place? Maybe; it was hard to tell what was on his mind. What a diplomat that man would have made! And what a poker player . . .

I hadn't meant to blurt out that stuff about Ilionis. Somehow the conversation had veered in that direction, and I had been carried along with the current. But I hoped that she had not told him what I really thought about the quest; no point in breaking his illusions now. Let the old man dream on, happily anticipating the mother-lode of all treasures . . . He would have to wake up to hard facts soon enough, God knows.

As for Ilsa, she strode along with her head bent, shoulders bowed under something more than the weight of her light pack. Why had I blurted out all those ugly things to her? Because I was beginning to fall in love with the girl and wanted to defend my honor before her? *Traitor* is an ugly label to have pasted on your forehead. But I had worn that label long enough to get used to it.

Along toward noon the Doctor came up to where I was leaning against a rock for a moment to catch my breath.

"Citizen, do you think we are in any present danger from these Moon Dragon warriors you mentioned? I notice how your gaze keeps straying to the top of the cliffs."

I shrugged. "They're up there somewhere, that's for sure. They'll find us sooner or later. And when they do, just let me do the talking. And keep Brother Konstantin away from the guns."

"Certainly, certainly!" He cleared his throat nervously. "Do you think we'll have trouble getting past them?"

"Not if they accept me for their Jamad Tengru."

"And . . . if they don't?"

"Then we'll have trouble. Lots of trouble. But we won't be alive long enough to have to worry about it," I said with a grim laugh.

"But I understood that all of the native clans recognized you as their holy sovereign."

"Well, the Low Clans do. I don't know about the High Clans," I admitted. "I've never met with them or ridden at their side into battle or shared *chardaka* under the Twin Moons."

"Is there any question that the High Clans, as you call them, will recognize your claim?"

"There's *always* a question, where the High Clans are concerned," I said shortly. "They are the proudest of a proud people and the oldest of an old race. They are very close to the Timeless Ones, the Martian gods who dwell in the underworld paradise of Yhoom, if you know your legends. They are second cousins to the gods; they are almost gods themselves. The archpriests and the prophets and great war leaders throughout history were drawn from the High Clans. Every Jamad for half a million years has been a High Clansman. Except for the last one, Thyoma, who died in my arms. And me, of course."

My words did not exactly reassure him. They were not meant to. When we met up with the war horde, I wanted him to be scared enough to do exactly what I told him to do. And to keep that bloody Ukrainian under control. I told him as much, and he hastened to assure me he would follow my orders. When we met the Riders.

We didn't have long to wait, as it turned out.

That evening we were worn out from a day of staggering through knee-deep sand, so we made camp early, even before sundown. The sky was still light as we started to set up the tents. Ilsa was holding the frame of one as I stretched the fabric tight and sealed it against air loss. Then her hands froze.

And she stifled a shriek.

I spun around, and there they were. Twenty . . . thirty . . . but I had no time to count them. My heart was in my throat, and my hands were sweating.

They were mounted on rangy, plateau-bred riding beasts, *slidars,* they call them. Ungainly, splay footed, awkward red beasts they are, but they move as silently as shadows sliding over the sand.

They were ranged along the cliff edge, where a long cantilene sloped down into the Rill. They had gathered swiftly, picking their way daintily on silent feet. And those who sat astride the great red *slidars* were silent too. Tall, grim-faced men with bleak, cold eyes and russet fur instead of hair.

They had swords, long, whip-bladed rapiers, but they hung scabbarded at their sides. In their hands were long slender hollow black tubes. I knew those tubes from of old, and a cold wind went up and down my spine.

"Cats!" said Bolgov in an explosive grunt. And true to type, he went for his gun. I slapped it from his hands, and I was not gentle about it.

"No guns, you fool," I said. "Those tubes are loaded with darts like hollow needles. They could put twenty needles in you before you could touch the trigger. And one dart is enough to kill you where you stand."

His eyes showed white around the eyeball. He was scared, and he showed it, and he hated having me see it. His lips writhed back in a snarl.

"You lousy coward—I could have had them by now! You may be afraid to stand and fight like a man, but I got—"

"If you haven't learned the difference between courage and idiocy yet, you're not going to get the lesson at my expense. You touch that gun again, and you're a dead man."

"Citizen Tengren, we'll do exactly as you say," the Doctor said haltingly. I have to hand it to the old boy; his voice shook a bit, but his eyes were steady.

"Just stand still and don't make any sudden moves of any kind," I said.

And I started to walk toward the cantilene. I was sweating hard; I could feel it running down my belly and under my arms. But I kept the fear out of my face and made it an expressionless mask.

I walked toward them, moving slow and careful, keeping my hands away from my sides, even though I wore no guns. Ten or twelve of them had the long slender tubes at their lips. They could kill me with a breath, I knew. I had seen those tubes in action. On a low-gravity planet with a thin, windless atmosphere, a blowgun is a weapon of fantastic range and accuracy.

Any one of the Riders could have brought down a sparrow on the wing at one hundred and seventy-five paces.

So I went slow, letting them see that I was coming.

It might have been the last walk I would ever take.

It surely seemed like the longest.

6. The Riders of Chun

They watched me with narrow, measuring eyes as I walked slowly across the open space toward the foot of the cantilene. When I was near the base, I raised my hands and made the Greeting and the Call to Parley.

That surprised them! They muttered among themselves and cast me odd looks. Few of the Hated Ones, the *F'yagha,* have ever bothered to learn the Signs; old Keshkuz had taught them to me, that endless winter we lay holed up in Tharsis, waiting for the White Hawk nation to muster its legions and ride to join us in the holy war.

One or two detached themselves from the rest and came down the long slope of the cantilene into the Rill. Gaunt, scarlet beasts stepping gingerly, riders leaning back in the high saddles against the steep angle. One of them was a grim, heavy-faced man in his middle years, his fur cap graying about the temples; the other a rangy, long-legged boy with eager, angry eyes, hot for blood.

A third followed at an amble; a fat little man, looking oddly soft and out of place among the lean warriors. He had a round, innocent face and merry eyes. A thirty-stringed *odyar* was slung across his shoulders.

I climbed the rocks to join them at the bottom of the slope. As I came up and took my stand, I made a gesture of courtesy and greeted them in the High Tongue.

They made me no answer. The older man sat his restive mount easily, looking me over from head to toe with narrow, thoughtful eyes.

As for the boy, he sat proudly, his smooth young face as fierce and as beautiful as a hawk's. The fingers of one hand played with the hilt of his sword. He was thirsty for my blood, that boy: eager to prove himself a warrior.

The fat little harper sat back in his high saddle, smiling

cherubically, eyes beaming with humor. He switched his *odyar* around, cradling it between his thighs, pudgy fingers drumming idly on the old polished wood.

The heavy-faced, graying man was clearly the one in authority here, for the others waited for him to speak first. His voice was harsh, and his tone peremptory.

"Now just what are you, *F'yagh,* that speak the Tongue and make the Signs as if you were of the People?" he demanded.

"I am of the People, as you say," I replied calmly. "Despite my birth. My name is Hnoma among the Nine Nations. I have shared water with Prince Thuu of the Red Mountain nation, and his brethren are my brethren. I rode to war under the Red Mountain banner when——"

The boy hissed like a spitting cat, and his eyes flashed.

"What madness do we hear?" he shrilled. "An Outworlder, riding to war against Outworlders? Is this not madness, Uncle Kuruk? Are we to listen to these lies?"

The heavy-faced man, Kuruk, reproved him sternly.

"Be silent, Chaka, or go back to the warriors and let men speak together."

"Still not his tongue, Lord," I said. "The question is one that needs answering. I have in truth turned from the ways of my people to follow your ways. My people have named me outcast and renegade. But what of that? 'A man must follow as his own heart bids him go.' "

The grim eyes of Kuruk lost a little of their frostiness.

"Well, you know the Old Poet, at least, *F'yagh!*" he said. "But here is a mystery: an Outworlder who speaks the Tongue and knows the Signs and quotes the sagas! Wonder upon wonder, surely. Can it be you know the Law as well? If you ride beneath the Red Mountain banner and have shared water with the Prince of that clan, then show me the sigil thereof."

"He wears it not, I'll wager!" the boy muttered, sneering at me with angry eyes. Those eyes dropped and smooth cheeks flushed as the lord turned a sharp glare upon the youth.

With slow fingers, being very careful to keep my hands in clear view, lest they suspect me of going for a gun, I unseamed my thermal suit, opened my shirt and laid my chest bare. I let them look at that which was inked deep in the flesh above my heart. Their eyes widened.

"*Hoya!* But you bear the marks of not one but four!" the lord exclaimed. "How is this? You claim the Four Nations as your brethren? Never have I heard of such a thing."

The boy cantered near, half-drawing his sword.

"The *F'yagh* is a cheap imposter and does not know the Laws!" he shrilled accusingly. "Let me slay him now, Kuruk, and the old man below. We will take the goods and the woman and leave the men head down, as a warning—"

"Eh, heh, brothers!"

A laughing, lazy voice spoke up. It was the moon-faced little man with the harp. They turned, I as well; his merry eyes laughed at us.

"This one has heard a tale, oh, a mad, mad tale!" he chuckled. "Of an Outworlder, tall and straight, broad shouldered and hard faced, with gray hair and wintry eyes . . . Oh, a mad tale they tell of this one! He turned against his own people, they tell, to ride with the Nations in holy war; he is brother to the Four Nations of the North, they say . . . but they are mad, quite mad, who tell it!"

His soft, lazy voice spun a strange spell. He held them mesmerized, the grim lord, the hot-eyed youth; they watched him, and they listened to him. He held the *odyar* on his broad lap as he talked in his laughing, breathless way, and his fingers wandered idly across the thirty strings, rousing a weird, careless music.

"They say he pitied Holy Thyoma in his cell and freed him of his chains. They say he rode out with him under the two moons, deep into the dustlands, so that the old man might rejoin his People and might come to the end of his days among the Nations . . . Oh, a mad tale, surely! They say the Holy One sickened from the tortures he had suffered, sickened there in the dustlands far from the camps of the Low Clans. And they tell that this tall Out-worlder tended Thyoma in his illness, as gently as a woman..."

The weird music crooned low and ached with sadness now.

"They say Thyoma died in his arms, blessing him, calling him brother, yea, even the *F'yagh*," laughed the moon-faced little man, while the harp moaned beneath his hands. "Even the Hated One, the accursed Outworlder, akin to they that plunder our sad world and rape our women and hunt us like dogs ... Why, the mad tale tells that ere he died and journeyed down to dark Yhoom and crossed the Bridge of Fire to lay his heart at the feet of the Timeless Ones, the Holy Thyoma set upon the Out-worlder's brows the Iron Crown itself and died with the last word of the Ritual upon his withered lips ... Oh, mad, mad, the tale they tell!"

Kuruk's eyes were wide in his grim face as he looked at me.

Under his breath he said faintly: "This one ... the ... *Jamad?*"

But the boy would have none of it. He spat, and his eyes were ugly.

"Lies, madness, and now blasphemy! I say, slay him and take the woman! Let fat Huw sing his crazy songs and gibber as he pleases; the gods touched him with the sacred madness, and he is mad, and his words cannot be trusted."

Kuruk measured me with wondering eyes.

"'Tis not Huw that made the tale, boy! I too have heard it. Outworlder, let us hear truth now. The time for lies is past. *Who are you?*"

It was gettting dark swiftly. I looked him straight in the eyes. "I am the one," I said. "The one of whom Huw speaks."

"They said you were taken under the walls of Omad," he said, breathing heavily. "They said the Hated Ones bore you off in chains for judgment, according to their law. *They said you died years ago!*"

"I live. And I have come back. To take up the sword again and to lead the People to freedom."

His breathing was hoarse in the stillness.

"If you are . . . what they say . . . then reveal yourself to me. Otherwise you die, Outworlder!"

They watched me as I slid the pack off my shoulders, eased it to the ground, and unseamed it. Kuruk watched with wonder and the beginnings of awe; Chaka with hatred in his eyes and a curious fear, as well. Fat Huw watched lazily, fingers wandering idly across the strings, making a tuneless music.

I heard them gasp as I drew out the ancient cloth. Even in the dimming light, the designs on the precious *yonka* were clear.

I raised the Iron Crown into view, and they stopped breathing.

The vague music stopped abruptly in a jangling discord, as I lifted it to my brows.

Starlight flashed dazzlingly in the great crystals set in the iron hoops. A tangle of rays, a blur of light, spun about my head like a crazy halo as I settled the Crown into place.

I turned my gaze upon them.

They were pale, the three of them, and fear was naked in their faces.

I assumed my Power and wrapped myself in it like a cloak before them.

My thought, magnified ten million times, projected into their minds like crashing thunder, rolling among the hills.

I am the Lord of Lords! And I am the Prince of Princes. Nine Nations ride in thunder at my heels, and nine banners go before me when I ride to war. Behold me in my Power, men of Chun, and fear me. For the Timeless Ones watch over my path, and this world is my domain, from the white pole of the north to the white pole of the south. I am the Jamad Tengru. There is no other.

A great sigh went among the warriors on the ridge, and they came down from their beasts and bowed all in a line, as a row of corn bows beneath the unseen passing of the wind.

"Lord . . ."

I looked down to where grim Kuruk knelt in the dust

before me, with the boy Chaka at his side, frightened now, and hungry for my blood no longer; and even fat Huw had scrambled down to his knees and knelt wheezing in the grit.

"Lord, we have threatened you with bronze, and we have named you with names of hatred and called you liar," said Kurik heavily, not daring to look at me. "Spare the young chieftain Chaka, who bade us to take your woman and to slay you. He is a worthless puppy and a boastful child, but he is a warrior of the Moon Dragon and my sister's son. Slay me, if it please you but let the boy live; let him live, that he may fight by your side in the holy wars."

"Get up, Kuruk," I said. "All of you, get up. No one shall die for a few hasty words. There will be a need for every sword when the Moon Dragon banner flies in the winds of war. Enough of us will shed our blood under the two moons, before we hold this world in our hands. Get up!"

He rose, grinning, wiping the dust from his knees.

The young chieftain rose also and stood shamefaced. There was a hang-dog look to him. I laughed and clapped his shoulder.

"Chaka! You look like a boy who has spat in the wind and finds his face wet. Be bold!"

The youth grinned, blushing, and his shining eyes were full of something I had not seen in a long time. A sort of hero worship; a kind of love.

"Yes, Lord," he said. And I knew he was mine from that moment to the death.

Old Huw chuckled and struck a wild chord from his harp.

"Eh, Lord . . . a mad world, when mad tales come true," he wheezed in his merry, lazy way.

Kuruk looked to me for instruction.

"How far is it to your camp?"

"Four hours' hard riding, Lord; we have not beasts enough for you and your people. But the warriors will be proud to walk in the dust while you honor their saddles."

"Not tonight. My friends and I have walked all day. Meet us here at dawn with fresh mounts, and we will go to your camping place together, for I must hold converse with your Prince."

He nodded. "Prince Kraa, my father, will deem himself blessed to lay his sword at your feet. I go, Lord."

I stood and watched them mount. They whirled about, raising their right arms in the warrior's salute, and were off in a billow of dust. And I came down to the camp very wearily.

The Doctor was pale and shaken, but jubilant.

"Good God, my boy! That was a tense moment . . . Why, my heart was in my mouth when they sprang off those scarlet animals. They *knelt* before you! An amazing sight! Simply amazing!"

Ilsa's face was full of wonder; Bolgov was sullen and subdued. The force of the Power had perhaps brushed them with the edges of its aura, but they had not heard the thought message as it thundered—being *F'yagha*.

"They'll be back at dawn with steeds for us," I said in a tired voice. "We'll go to their camping place tomorrow and get guides to take us to the site. Now let's eat and get as much rest as we can. Tomorrow will be a busy day."

Something woke me suddenly. I cannot put a name to it: a tension in the air, to which subtler senses than the known and numbered five responded. But I came from the depths of sleep to full, tingling wakefulness all at once, like a cat.

There was a strange silence. I glanced at my watch and saw that it was full morning. Something was wrong, or the others would have awakened me ere this. I dressed in haste, fingers trembling over the fastenings of my thermal suit. Then I unseamed the tent, drew back the flap, and stepped out into the wash of full sunlight—

And stopped dead!

Two thousand silent warriors sat their steeds, drawn up in two perfect ranks.

They formed a double lane that led straight from the front of my tent to where an old, old man with silver fur stood facing me from a considerable distance.

It was like a weird vision, the ranks of motionless men,

the huge scarlet beasts, old banderoles hung from long slender spears, all bathed in the sunlight, suspended in an aching silence.

I looked away. Bolgov and Ilsa and Keresny stood by their tents, all frozen in silence. There was awe upon their faces: fear in the eyes of the black-bearded Ukrainian, wonder in the pale visage of the blond girl and nervousness and excitement in the Doctor's lean, aristocratic face.

I walked forward slowly, down the lane of mounted warriors who watched me pass with impassive features. I held my head high and my shoulders back and did my best to walk like a king. Grit and pebbles crunched under my boots; I felt the unnerving pressure of hundreds of eyes upon me.

As I neared the old man, I could see that he was truly aged, aged even beyond the longevity usual to his race. The fur on his head was pure silver; the flesh of his face had fallen away, and the fine bones showed through. But his eyes were keen and alert. They studied me from shadowy hollows as I came striding up to where he stood, huddled in splendid robes more ancient even than was he, threadbare in places and faded by centuries.

I came to a halt before him. The silence stretched taut around us. He peered deeply into my eyes, and as his wise, sharp gaze probed me I felt ghostly tendrils touch the outer fringes of my mind ever so gently.

He was of the Old Race, and something of the Power lingered within him too. The blood of ancient dynasties of kings flowed in those shrunken veins, attenuated, but true bred.

I think he read authority in my eyes. I think he felt the aura of my Power about me, which rises to its peak only when I don the crown. His eyes widened; his intent gaze faltered and fell.

The old prince went slowly to his knees before me.

He leaned forward and kissed the dirt between my boots.

And as one man, two thousand warriors flung themselves from their saddles into the dust.

I leaned forward and raised the old man to his feet and kissed him between the eyes to seal the peace between us.

The warriors sprang to their feet. They brandished their spears in the air joyously. There was one great, crashing shout—

"Hai-yaa! Jamad!"

I smiled at Prince Kraa, and he returned my smile, for all that tears trembled in his old eyes. He touched my hand.

"Lord, command us: the Riders of Chun are your servants," he said in a quavering voice.

I shook my head. "They are my comrades-in-arms," I said. "For too long have the warriors of the Moon Dragon nation dwelt apart from their brethren. The Four Nations rode at my back in the holy war against the Hated Ones. But nine share this world between them. When next the war banner flies beneath The Twin Moons, *five* nations, at least, shall follow it."

Fire flashed in his eyes. He drew himself up proudly, like an old warhorse.

"Jamad, it shall be even so!"

I felt the pressure of other eyes upon me.

I turned to stare directly into a cold, malignant gaze. They were cold and black and beady, those eyes, and there was suspicion and distrust in them. The man was a priest, I knew, for his head was shaven and his hunched, hideous body was wrapped in voluminous robes of virulent green.

I felt an instinctive revulsion and recoiled as one might shrink back from a venomous serpent. The priest recognized my emotion and laughed. An ugly, hard laugh, devoid of warmth or humor. But in truth, the priest was hideous, monstrous, terribly deformed. Some spinal defect had twisted his body until he hunched as if half-crushed under a terrible weight. And he was no more than half my height—a dwarf—the first such I had seen among the People. His face was seamed with deeply carved lines; a cold sneer was stamped about the lipless gash of his frog-like mouth, and his eyes were set far apart under beetle brows. His face was a mask of malignant fury and despair and self-loathing.

All this I took in at a glance.

The old Prince gestured. "Dhu, priest of the Timeless Ones, hereditary Guardian of the Gates of Yhoom."

I nodded curtly to the little monster of a pontiff and exchanged a few more words with the old Prince, telling him we would return with him and his legion to their base.

The dwarfed priest cleared his throat raspingly and cocked a contemptuous eye at my companions.

" 'We'? Go the accursed *F'yaga* with us to the city?"

I tried to cow him with an imperious glance, but in vain.

"My . . . *friends* . . . go with me. Unless the priest Dhu has any objection?"

He shrugged elaborately, deformed shoulders lifting. "Not I! The Lord may bring his dogs with him as he wills."

The Prince turned on him sharply. "Enough, priest! You shame us before the Jamad; his brethren are our brethren, while the world lasts. I will suffer no insolence, on my honor!"

The dwarf bowed obsequiously as I turned away.

But all the way back to where the Doctor and the others waited, I felt his cold, ugly eyes at the back of my neck.

7. The Gates of Farad

The *slidar* is a beast unique to Mars and cannot easily be compared to anything Earthside. It is a little larger than a terrene horse and has four legs and a long, arched neck, but there the resemblance stops. For the *slidar* is a reptile, scaled, fanged, snake tailed. Yet in its gaunt, big-shouldered awkwardness, bony and ungainly, it reminds many Earthmen of the camel.

It runs with a shambling, loping stride, hence its name:

for *slidar* means "loper" in the Tongue. Few Earthmen master the art of riding the beasts or feel easy in the saddle. But my companions managed it, although Bolgov's panic was evident and even laughable. He clutched the high saddle bow in a deathlike grip and paled under his swarthy tan, cursing volubly all the way.

Ilsa had learned the equestrian art at fashionable riding schools and adapted to the rolling stride of her mount with comparable ease. Even the Doctor managed to look graceful in the saddle.

The Chun warriors bundled our gear for us, loaded it on the backs of pack *slidars,* and we rode up the slope of the cantilene to the crest of the cliffs and set off due north across the top of the plateau.

Here all was crumbling, dry rock with yellow, dust-fine sand accumulating in the hollows. Nothing grew here but tough lichens and occasional patches of scabby moss. The tableland was scoured clean, an expanse of pitted, naked rock, pockmarked with the fumaroles of gas geysers.

Ilsa rode at my side. She could hardly manage to keep her eyes off our escort. I repressed a grin of amusement, for I well understood her amazement. For the desert world reserves yet a third surprise for its visitors: the People themselves.

Few Earthmen who have not seen the People realize how thoroughly human they are. True, the native Martians are, on the whole, taller and more leanly built than we are; lighter of bone and broader in the chest, to accommodate oxygen-storage cells to live in their rarified atmosphere. True, also, their heads, the backs of their hands, and chest and throat are covered, not with hair, but with a fine, silken fur, generally russet colored and forming a remarkably efficient natural insulation against heat loss. True, as well, that their eyes are larger than ours and with wider pupils, in compensation for the lesser amount of sunlight their dim world receives. It is these subtle peculiarities of eye and furcap, a certain gliding grace of motion, and the copper-amber of their pigmentation that instinctively remind us of cats and has earned them the appellation *Catmen.*

But these are only superficial differences and mean little. The racial variations of Earth itself are greater—the epicanthic fold above the eyes of the Mongoloid race, the woolly hair and ebon pigmentation of the Negroid. But surface oddities aside, the People are startlingly human, human where it really matters.

In the blood chemistry and down in the genes and chromosomes, they are—*men*.

At first all you notice is the amber skin, the russet fur, the large, black eyes of glittering obsidian. But before long, if you have no prejudices and certain powers of observation, you find yourself thrilling with awe and wonder at how recognizably human—at how genuinely *earth human*—they really are.

And those minor oddities of pigmentation and eye and hair somehow blend together: they fit somehow; they look —right. It comes over you with a weird shiver of mysterious awe that they could almost be a lost division of mankind . . . one more race, like the black, the brown, the yellow and the white . . . a race somehow lost or mislaid or strayed curiously afar in time's forgotten dawn.

When Christoffsen first got here and made contact with the White Hawk nation, he recorded with amazement and wondering speculation in his journal the essential *humanness* of the Martians. The very last thing the scientists had expected to find on the desert world was an intelligent indigenous race: *that* hoary old dream was a primitive plot concept that even the science fiction writers of the last century had long since abandoned. But there they were . . .

Even today the experts have no workable theory to explain it. Any number of schools of thought exists on the subject. The followers of Cantwell argue that *homo sapiens* is simply the only practical design for intelligent life. They muster impressive biological reasons why any race that is intended to develop a high civilization *has* to evolve into an erect, warm-blooded, oxygen-breathing, mammalian biped with binocular vision, an opposing thumb, and a carbon-based body chemistry. But they are really building their arguments out of a self-justification; if the only two civilized races yet discovered share these similarities, it takes on the weight of natural law.

The followers of Diego de Renza, however, discount the whole argument due to insufficient evidence. De Renza points out that any G-type star is likely to have its own planetary system, and that the chances of life evolving on some of them are statistically overwhelming. Perhaps a million planets in the galaxy are inhabited, he teaches, and when we have encountered a few hundred more, then— and *only* then—can we start talking about natural law.

The anthropologists, and some of the more mystical archaeologists, are rather evenly divided in their opinion that some lost, forgotten, preglacial civilization colonized both worlds before succumbing to the Ice Age. One school of thought argues that Earth was colonized from Mars. The other, that Mars was settled by prehistoric Earthmen. And there is even a splinter group to claim that both planets were merely colonies of the mythical fifth planet, Aster, which destroyed itself in a nuclear war and broke up to form the Asteroid Zone.

The one indisputable fact in all this morass of opinion is that nobody really knows for sure.

Before the sun had reached the zenith, we approached the walls of Farad.

I was surprised to discover that the Moon Dragon nation was a city-dwelling people. Most of the others had regressed down the long slope from urban civilization to the edges of barbarism. The Martians had once been a world empire. Ages passed, and they split into national units; with more ages the nations disintegrated first into city-states and then all the way back to wandering nomadic warrior clans.

This too had fascinated the scholars and the scientists, giving them exciting raw material for more theory spinning. It would seem that million-year-old civilizations tended to repeat the march of history—from tribe to empire—in reverse at the close of their history.

But Prince Kraa's people yet dwelt within the walls of one of the age-old Martian cities. Outside of the little-known Golden Lion nation, which lives somewhere in the polar regions of the north, none of the Nine Nations still clung to urban ways.

The city, therefore, was still inhabitable and even in repair. As we came riding up the long paved way, lined with those peculiar Martian sphinxes that look so much like enormous crouching insects of stone, we could see that the great outer wall was still standing, and we glimpsed impossibly slim towers soaring beyond.

Dr. Keresny was alive with scholarly enthusiasm, his eyes sparkling with excitement. His lips moved slightly, as if he was already phrasing out the opening paragraphs of the monograph he would write when all this was over. I grinned a trifle grimly: at least he would take that much back with him. The treasure might be an empty myth, but here was a discovery of considerable scientific value.

As we drew nearer, we could see that our first impressions of immemorial Farad were untrue. Once it had been an immense metropolis—the Babylon or the Carthage of antique Mars, perhaps. But that was very long ago. A million years had passed since that long-gone and glorious day, and the once-mighty people who still inhabited the city had shrunken into a pitiful remnant of what they had once been. Entire quarters of the city lay crumbling in ruin; sand had drifted in to choke superb boulevards lined with the chipped and broken eidolons of time-vanquished emperors.

Only a small portion of the city was still inhabited and still kept in some semblance of repair, and that was the *caravanserai* area near the main gates. Far back, crowning a hilly height, the moldering pile of rubble that had once been the magnificent palace complex of ancient Farad slumped in wreckage. There, perhaps as recently as the Pleistocene, the remote ancestors of Prince Kraa had reigned in sumptuous grandeur.

Now their descendants dwelt in a three-story stone building they might have considered little better than a hovel.

But the wall still stood, its megalithic stone blocks, each weighing as much as a ton, so perfectly smoothed as to fit together without the use of mortar. The gates were built on the grand scale. Soaring pylons of black marble rose to the moon, like black obelisks, and the hieroglyphs were still visible upon their faces, although geological epochs had passed since they had been newly carved.

The portals themselves were immense doors of cast bronze. Once they had been sheathed in gold plating, or perhaps covered with something akin to gold leaf. For here and there the shining metal, paper thin, still remained upon the ináccessible upper edges.

The gates stood open, and we rode between them, entering upon a broad avenue lined with perhaps three thousand men and women and children. We rode in triumph up that avenue; banners broke from window ledges, balconies, rooftops. Again I drank in the many-throated thunder of the *hai-yaa,* the Salute of Kings.

The Great House opened upon a great square like an old Roman forum. Along its front ran a great colonnade with a sort of *stoa* behind the row of stately columns. The arched portal was supported by two stone titans like caryatids. It was grand, surely, but the ages had not left it unscathed. Deep-cut glyphs adorned the massive pillars, and the passage of centuries had worn and pitted the sleek marble until the glyphs could scarcely be read.

We drew up before the House of Kraa, and there in ceremonial robes stood grizzled Kuruk to greet us, his heavy face beaming. The boy, Chaka, stood with him. He had eyes only for me, the boy, in all that princely throng.

I caught his eyes and called him to me with a gesture. Then I told the priests and chamberlains of the House to stand away, and let the boy hold the bridle of my *slidar* as I dismounted.

It was an honor, of course. His eyes shone with pride, and much the same light was in the proud gaze of Kuruk.

And so it was I came to Farad . . .

A magnificent suite was placed at my disposal. My companions were to have rooms below, among the cubicles of the slaves. I told the priests and chamberlains that my friends would stay with me, and as there was plenty of room, this was no inconvenience. I thought it wiser to keep us all together; I could not see Ilsa curled shivering on a pallet, and it seemed prudent to keep Bolgov away from the natives as far as could be managed. His ignorant dislike of the People and his explosive temper might get Keresny and Ilsa in trouble. I wanted no duels or blood feuds to complicate our relations with our host.

While we unpacked our gear, the Doctor was bubbling over with scholarly excitement. In truth the room was like something painstakingly reconstructed for a museum. The worn, faded old tapestries had been bright and new before Babylon was born; the tessellated pave had been designed by artisans before Egypt emerged from the Neolithic. The inscriptions on the marble walls were in a language so ancient that no one alive could read them. The very air was sweet with incense burned tens of thousands of years ago.

"My boy, this is fantastic! A living city, still inhabited after all these ages! My colleagues would be mad with jealousy if they knew I were here. Why, Le Corbeiller would give his right arm . . . And we are on the right track, by all the gods!"

"What do you mean?"

"The treasure, of course. Didn't you notice those black obelisks that framed the city gate?"

I shrugged. "I saw them, yes. But I didn't notice anything in particular out of the ordinary. Why?"

"The *inscriptions,* my boy! Do you mean to say you rode past them without reading them?"

I nodded.

He leaned close, eyes glistening.

"Thank heaven one of us kept his wits about him!" he chortled. "We filed through slowly enough for me to translate them, roughly, of course, but I managed to grasp the essential message."

His voice dropped to an awed, and somehow gloating, whisper, and he repeated the inscription:

" '*Here stands Farad, that guards the road to Ilionis, the Gateway of the Gods.*' "

And it was then, I think, that a strange forboding touched my heart . . .

That evening the Prince gave a great feast in our honor.
Lord Kuruk entered the suite, bearing ceremonial robes
for all of us. My companions would be gowned in the blue
robes of guests; but for the Jamad there were garments of
another sort.

The heavy man opened a case of fragrant winewood
and drew them out with careful, reverent hands.

"The Queens of Farad wove them over a thousand generations ago," he said, "when the world was young."

Ilsa drew in her breath, marveling.

The robes were delicate tapestries whereon were pic-
tured scenes from the Book of Kings; each scene was done
with ten thousand stitches, so fine that the eye could
scarce make out any single stitch. They were done of royal
silks, in colors so rich and vivid that the very blending and
dyeing of them had been a lost art for countless centuries.

Any museum in the System would trade half a dozen
Rembrandts for the thing: it was a miracle of great art.

And I was to wear it for dinner!

Kuruk bowed and left. We cleansed ourselves of dust
and began to prepare ourselves.

Ilsa shivered. "They hate us so much! I could feel it in
their eyes, as they escorted us here. All but you . . . They
love you . . . But you are a Hated One too!"

"I was once. Now I am the Jamad."

She regarded me curiously. "That means 'emperor,'
doesn't it?"

"More or less. God-king or priest-king, something like
that. Sort of like pope and emperor all in the same man.
You see, the Martian people are divided into nine great
clan-groups, very frequently at each other's throats. They
are united only in their veneration of the Jamad Tengru. I
am temporal monarch and spiritual leader at once, and the
spiritual part comes in because they regard me as the in-
carnation of all the Jamad Tengri who have reigned before
me since time began . . ."

"Not without reason, though," Ilsa said slyly.

I nodded reluctantly; I disliked speaking of these matters.

"The Iron Crown," I said. "You saw the great crystals on it. Well, they are thought records of a kind. A thought record, like the one your grandfather found, is a paper-thin wafer of metallic crystal, imperishable and indestructible. The crystals in the Crown are of the same substance, but with thousands of times the capacity."

I could see she understood none of this.

"Each Jamad wears the Crown when in council or enthroned in state or when dispensing justice. The Crown is attuned to his thoughts, and the crystals record what is in his mind in those moments of high decision. When each Jamad dies, he selects his own successor and attunes the Crown to that person. The crystals bear the imprint of his mind, the sum total of his experience and something of his character and personality too. With his Power upon him the next Jamad has access to all the knowledge, the statesmanship, and the wisdom of all the emperors who reigned before him . . . He *is* all of those wise and great men, in a very real sense. And thus all Mars regards him as holy."

"However did they come to choose you?" she asked bluntly. Bolgov sniggered at the expression on my face. Keresny smoothly interceded.

"The story goes that the Colonial Administration took the last native Jamad into, ah, I believe the euphemism is 'protective custody.' For his own good, of course," he explained.

I smiled without mirth. "Yes; just as Cortez imprisoned Montezuma for his own 'protection.' And made the Aztecs ransom him by filling a room with gold. Thyoma was a saintly old man and frail. He could not believe the Administrator General was as treacherous as his counselors warned; he delivered himself into the hands of the Hated Ones."

My face was bleak, I suppose. She shrank from the look in my eyes.

"They tortured him with electroshock and drugged him with neopentothal. They were after treasure, of course. But Earthside drugs react unpredictably on Martians. They were killing him," I said softly. "So I set him free, killing a guard or two in the process. I stole a skimmer and got him out; but he was dying, inch by inch. We holed up in some ruins, and I did what I could for the old man. But it was soon over."

Her eyes clung to my face.

"Before a Jamad dies, he has to bestow the Crown on someone. If he dies without doing so—without performing the Ritual that attunes the telepathic receptors of the Crown to the mental frequencies of the next Jamad—then the Crown dies too. And can never be used again. The crystals would go dead, and all that those million-year-old memories, all the wisdom of ancient kings, would be lost forever."

I drew a deep breath.

"I was the only one with him as he lay dying. So he passed the Crown to—*me.*"

"And they . . . accepted you, an Earthman?" she asked in a faint, wondering voice.

"Yes. But not easily. The priests were against it. But the warriors learned that I had slain my own people to set the old man free and that I had tended him as he lay dying. *They* named me Jamad, and the Princes of the nations swore fealty to me. I was willing to pass the Crown along to another and to perform the Ritual for him . . . for who was I, to claim the empire of Mars?"

"But they would not let you," Keresny said softly. I nodded slowly.

"They refused. They said that his Power had been upon him when he chose me as Jamad. They said the wisdom of a million years of royalty spoke through his lips in that moment and that the Timeless Ones had selected me to be the deliverer who would mediate between the two worlds."

I laughed a bit wildly.

"I was of Earth blood, but my own people called me 'outlaw' and 'traitor,' and my own government disowned me! I was the Jamad Tengru of all Mars, but no clan or nation called me brother! Alone in a limbo of two worlds, and I—I—am supposed to bring them together in peace!"

"But they did accept you and came to love you!"

"In time, yes. I tried to bring the claim of the People before the Mandate, to win simple justice for them. All we wanted was self-rule; the Earthmen could stay, the Colonies could have their land. Mars was big enough for both races, I said. But they refused to recognize my authority. They put a price on my head and tried to hunt me and those who rode with me. So there was no other course but to raise the war banner against all the occupation force, CA cops and simple Colonists as well. First, it was only Prince Thuu's people, the Red Mountain clans, who fought at my side against the Earthmen. But before very long, the White Hawk nation joined us, and toward the end of it all, four nations had joined me in the holy war. We came surprisingly close to winning too, but the Hated Ones were too strong for us. We had nothing but bronze swords and spears and the strength of our hatred."

I laughed bitterly.

"That doesn't count for much, against beta cannons and fission bombs."

"But now you have come back, and new supporters have joined your cause," the Doctor reminded me softly.

I nodded. "Yes. Prince Kraa has recognized me, and the warriors of the Moon Dragon nation will join the four nations, and the war can begin again."

"And where will it all end this time?" the girl asked, somberly. "In more fighting and killing—in more dying?"

"Yes. But this time, before the war banner is lifted, I will enlist all of the nations. Prince Kraa will dispatch emissaries to those nations that have not yet joined in my cause. When we are done with this sorry business of the Ilionis treasure, I will raise all of Mars in a holy war. And we outnumber the Earthmen by many hundreds to one."

Keresny nodded sympathetically. "But they still have beta cannons and fission bombs," he said.

"True. But this time they will not take me alive, thus ending the battle. This time we will fight to the last living warrior. And I can't believe that even the Mandate will be able to stand before the massed weight of public opinion. Genocide is the dirtiest word in the lexicon of politics. They would have to murder a whole world to stop us."

I broke off as the door swung inward, displaying a pompous chamberlain.

It was time for the feast.

8. The Hall of the Moons

The feasting was held in a vast, column-thronged chamber that resembled the great hypostyle hall of Karnak at Thebes.

The Hall of the Moons, it was called. Two beaten discs of ancient silver adorned one wall, their dully gleaming surfaces fantastic with curling arabasques and complicated symbols. The People have accumulated a famous ephemeris of the lunar cycles, for to them, with their great, light-gathering eyes, the dim, small, hurtling moons are visible. And from the complex orbital patterns the twin moons weave, their sorcerers and shamans foretell the future. The science of the moons is to the People what astrology once was to the primal nations of the Earth (and still is to some benighted souls).

We strode into the hall to a crash of slim trumpets. The scene was one of stupendous and barbaric splendor. A veritable forest of immense red marble pillars soared far above our heads, supporting a lofty, vaulted ceiling lost in gloomy shadows. The pillars were carved with spiraling lines of antique inscriptions; here within the Great House the weatherings of time had worked less destruction on such monuments of the past, and the ancient pigments were still visible, for faint traces of rich colorings could be glimpsed in the graved glymphs.

Basketwork cressets of hard bronze cupped smokeless white fires, dazzling and odorless. There is little wood on Mars and little enough oxygen whereby to burn wood; but the People have found a chemical substitute, derived from the oil of certain common mosses, which ignites with flameless brilliance when combined with a powdered mineral we have yet to identify.

Several hundred of the lords and nobles of the Moon Dragon sat on ritual cushions before ankle-high slab tables of carved stone. They wore ceremonial feasting robes of brilliant hues, and the scenic effect of the massed nobles in their glittering finery, under the blaze of the cressets, was savage and opulent.

My companions were delighted at the warmth of the room, for great fires roared on stone grates and the steamy vapor of broiling meats filled the air with succulent odors and robbed it of its bitter chill. They were even more delighted when I advised them that they could safely remove their respirators. The atmosphere of Mars is thin and oxygen poor, of course, but it is no less breathable than that of the Himalayan heights or the great Andean plateau. It is the intense cold and the terrible dryness of the air that are so injurious to the lungs of Earthmen as to require the use of respirators. These condense the air which passes through them to a more breathable thickness and also heat and moisten it.

The deep-throated trumpet call died in echoes far overhead as we entered the hall and took the places indicated by the chamberlain. The hundreds who had risen to salute me at my entrance sank in a deep bow as I strode down the broad lane between the tables with my companions behind me as a sort of entourage.

I was guided to the High Seat of Honor on a broad dais of yellow marble with many steps. My chair was a capacious, thronelike thing of very ancient black wood which rose higher than the place of the Prince, who stood to welcome me. Keresny and Ilsa and Bolgov were given places of lesser honor on a lower step of the dais.

I noted sidewise glances and mutterings, and a certain hostility gleamed in the eyes of many of the nobles and chieftains as they saw that my companions were of the *F'yagha*, the Hated Ones. There was nothing that could be done about this, and I suppose the reaction was only natural, considering how much the People have suffered at the hands of the Earthmen. But I did not fear any open gesture of unfriendliness, and I felt that the stares and mutterings would pass, as indeed they did. For hospitality is a holy virtue among the People, and guest right a sacred obligation of honor.

A cold goblet of cut amethyst crystal was ceremoniously set into my hands by the Prince himself, who took up an identical goblet. Then with great solemnity, as a hush fell over the feasting throng, the fat chamberlain poured into our twin goblets a clear fluid. We drank together, he and I.

It was water—pure, cold water, rarer and more precious than any wine. Now I had "shared water" with Prince Kraa, as I had shared it with Thuu and Mha and Yatha and Eonnah, also Princes of Nations. And in so doing, a pact of friendship and brotherhood was sealed between us that only death could rend asunder.

He had yet to lay his sword at my feet, however, in the Vow of Fealty.

The precious water bottle was removed, and the goblets taken away. Cups of green jade were given us and were filled with wine. I saluted my water friend and drank deeply. The wine was thin and pale and golden, with honeyed fire at its heart, and it sang with delicious vigor through my veins like the rarest and most superb of champagnes.

Then the feast began; an endless variety of highly spiced meats, porcelain cups of steaming broth swimming with precious herbs, pickled roots and tubers, candied fruits from the Wetlands, and sugared pastries passed before us, borne on the shoulders of out-clan slaves on huge platters of gold and silver. And there were goblets of that curious and very precious blue-green metal peculiar to Mars, which became all the rage for jewelry back on Earth after Christoffsen returned home with the first sample. Martium they call it.

I saw Bolgov's eyes glitter with greed as smoking meats were offered to us on a platter of solid Martium worth twenty years' salary to one of his profession. He accepted a plate of small cubes of sweet white meat from the priceless platter, and I smiled as he gobbled them hungrily, eyes following the sheen of the metal.

"Delicious, isn't it, Brother Konstantin?"

He grunted. "Not bad."

"Yes, beautifully spiced. It's sand snake, of course . . ."

His face purpled, and he spat the mouthful into his napkin as I chuckled.

There were twenty-three courses and nine wines, ending with a brandy like liquid gold.

Musicians played between the tables, using instruments that few Earthmen ever see save in temple frescoes. Keresny followed them with fascinated eyes. The music was all composed of wailing minor notes, rather like Arab music, and the ringing of little silver chimes made a weird, tuneless counterpoint. Bolgov shifted restlessly, guzzling down the precious brandy; even Ilsa fidgeted a little, and I could not blame her. For all that my heart belonged to this desert world, even I did not understand her native music!

A fat chamberlain conducted the phases of the feast. As the musicians passed, he rang his heavy silver crozier against the marble pave and summoned the dancing girls with an imperious gesture.

They were slim and young, with tawny copper flesh, and their bare bodies writhed with boneless grace through a gliding sequence of alluring postures that were the very essence of all that is voluptuous. And they were nude beneath a thin layer of purple gauze, with gems woven through the night-black falls of their silken hair.

Bolgov ogled them with hot, hungry eyes. The Doctor took in the scenery with a twinkle in his eye, and the amused smile of a connoisseur. Ilsa, however, sat stiff with disapproval, her face flushed and eyes averted. I grinned, inhaled the magnificent brandy, and admired the dance.

The old Prince and Lord Kuruk, his only son, sat near me on the high place, but we exchanged few words during the feast itself, as the People considered it most rude to hold a conversation during a meal. I saw that the little dwarf-pontiff shared the crest of the dais with us and stuffed himself greedily, although he did not touch any of the wines. From time to time he shot me a glance eloquent of cold malignity, but I did not deign to return his look. I found myself wondering yet again at the reason for his obvious hatred of me.

True, the ancient priesthood of Mars has always been at odds with the great hereditary Princes, but the Jamad is above all such rivalries. Or so I had always supposed.

Once we were done eating, I broached the subject of our coming to Prince Kraa. I was as diplomatic as possible about it and as vague as I dared to be concerning the exact nature of our quest, but even so, the Prince was disturbed to learn that we sought to find the Lost City of Ilionis.

I tried to explain our motives, presenting them as something nobler than a squalid hunt for gold and jewels. I attempted to get across the notion of a scientific expedition, but this proved too subtle and alien for the old man to readily grasp. The People have fallen very far from the heights their splendid civilization once achieved, and the technological skills that enabled their ancestors to perfect such sophisticated artifacts as the thought records has long since become lost. The very concept of science itself is difficult to convey to them, and the Tongue lacks even a word for a scientist.

"The silver-haired one among my companions," I explained carefully, "is a Doctor. In the tongue of the Hated Ones that denotes a student of the ancient arts, a seeker after the lost wisdom of past ages. He would study the records of the achievements of your remote ancestors and set these matters down in writing, so that other men may learn thereof, thus adding to the store of their knowledge."

Kraa was baffled that a man should so spend his days and inquired seriously if Keresny was in good health.

"Surely, the *Dok-i-tar* has his women and the hunt and the wars of his people," he said dubiously. "He is not a priest, that one—a *kaffarh?*"

I strove to stifle a grin: a *kaffarh* is one who has been deprived (through drugs) of the use of certain organs and has thus lost his ability to enjoy one of the sensual prerogatives of a male, the better to perform his priestly or oracular duties without the distractions of the flesh. A gelding, you might say.

"No, the Doctor is a 'whole man'—but a man of great wisdom and deep learning," I said.

Kraa gave it up with a shrug. But he was unhappy at the thought of our questing after the Lost City.

"How shall the *Dok-i-tar* find the place of Ilionis? No man can truly say he knows the way. Many there be who say it is but a fable and not a thing of fact. Never have I heard a man tell the way to that place. Even we who dwell here in Farad, which the old songs say doth guard the road to Lost Ilionis—as is inscribed upon the pillars of the city gates—know naught of that place."

"He believes he has found the road thither," I said. And then I described the direction and the distance we intended to travel. I broke off suddenly, noting the dismay written large upon his features.

"Lord, that is beyond the boundaries of the *Hualokka*, the Sacred Land! No warrior of the Riders of Chun would trespass beyond the stone pillars that mark the borders of that land!"

His face was worried, and his voice was troubled. I tried to soothe him, reluctant to impose my authority as Jamad upon the will of my host and a warrior king I hoped would join me as an ally. But if I could not win his aid willingly, I would have to command him; for we needed his help; we could never make the march on foot across the bleak plateau alone.

"Nothing will be disturbed in that land," I said quietly. "The Doctor will look, will study, will observe. The holy peace of Ilionis will not be broken; neither will its treasure, if there indeed be treasure, be looted of so little as a single coin or one small gem."

It was dirt on my tongue to have to lie to the old man, and inwardly I breathed a curse on Josip Keresny and his damnedable treasure hunt. And most devoutly did I wish that there should indeed be no treasure at all and no city either. For Keresny and Bolgov could not be persuaded to leave the treasure intact, the vault unplundered; and how could I, the Jamad, be a party to such a sacrilege as the looting of the holiest place on Mars?

When I had first agreed on this thing, I had believed

without question that Lost Ilionis was a baseless fabrica-
tion—the El Dorado of Mars—and no more.

Now I was not so certain. For the distress in the voice
of Kraa was eloquent testimony.

He shook his head wonderingly. "Lord, my fathers and
my fathers' fathers have held all of the *Hualokka* sacrosanct since time began. And yet you are my Jamad, and
your whim is my law . . . Nay, stronger even than the Law
is your will! *Aiii!* These be heavy matters to decide."

It was then the capricious Fates took a hand.

For the dwarf-priest Dhu had been leaning near to
catch our words. Now his beady eyes flashed, and he
threw up his hands in a display of righteous indignation.

"Do I hear true, O Prince?" he shrilled. "The *F'yagha*
would have you lead them into the Sacred Land? To set
foot there is an affront to the very spirits of your sacred
ancestors, and it is to spit in the faces of the Timeless
Ones themselves!"

Kraa's face hardened.

"Be silent, priest, when Princes confer!" he snapped.
"If we require the opinions of the priesthood, we will in-
vite them."

The hunchback was not intimidated by this.

"Yet still I say these things are blasphemy—utter blasphemy!" he insisted. "And a *true* Jamad, a Jamad of the
ancient blood, would know that this is Law. The *F'yagh*
Jamad may wear the Crown and boast the name, but he is
an Outworlder and doubly forbidden to set foot on the soil
of the Sacred Land."

Some intuition told me to keep silent and let the two of
them fight this out. So I kept my face impassive; little Dhu
cast a gloating eye in my direction to see how I was taking
this and seemed the slightest bit disconcerted by my ap-
parent serenity and composure. As for the Prince, he was
wavering.

Dhu sensed his triumph. He drew himself up to the
most commanding height he could manage and delivered
the *coup de grace* in a scathing tones of withering contempt:

"But the *F'yagh* you name Jamad is but an imposter, little learned in the ways and lore of the People. Imagine! He searches for Ilionis, lost Ilionis, the city of the treasure; but were he truly a master of the ancient lore, he would know that Ilionis is but a legend and no more. It does not exist; it is only a story, only a myth out of lost ages!"

Prince Kraa's face was grim, and he cast me a dubious glance.

On a lower step of the dais, fat, moon-faced little Huw had lolled all this while. He was somewhat the worse for all the tankards of wine he had taken aboard: his round face was flushed, and his eyes twinkled with mirth. It would seem he had eavesdropped on this scene of confrontation.

"Eh, lords," he wheezed, "but if this Ilionis does not exist at all, well . . . I wonder how it can be that merely to seek for it is blasphemy and sacrilege?"

It was as if his casual words, drawled in a lazy and laughing voice, had dropped into the scene like a bombshell.

Dhu flushed; his wide, froglike mouth, which had opened to drive home yet another nail in the coffin of my hopes, hung open for a moment, as the vindictive little monster suddenly realized he had put his foot in it.

By a miracle I kept my face straight, managing to retain my expression of calm composure. But the Prince's eyes flashed, and his lips curled in a little smile as the implications of the fat minstrel's remarks began to occur to him.

Dhu faltered, wavered; Prince Kraa eyed him blandly; and I began to understand that little or no love was lost between the Prince and priest. It was the age-old struggle for supremacy, acted out here in Farad as it has been played on many another stage across the face of this old, old world. And fat Huw, either intentionally or through sheer accident, had just given Kraa splendid ammunition to win this round of the old battle.

"Your opinion on this point, O Dhu?" he inquired in a soft, purring voice. "If there is no such place as Ilionis, to which truth you yourself attest, then how can the searching for it be considered sacrilege?"

"I . . . uh . . . it . . . is sacrilege to attempt that which the Timeless Ones, in their infinite wisdom, have forbidden," the priest stammered lamely.

"Then the Timeless Ones have forbade men to search for that which is *nowhere* and which, therefore, cannot possibly be found?" the Prince inquired blandly.

Dhu shut his mouth sulkily, eyes ugly.

Below, where he sprawled on plump cushions, Huw chuckled. The little hunchback snarled, flushing.

With an expression of smug amusement, the Prince watched Dhu as the hunchback thought furiously, eyes roaming desperately about in search of an inspiration or a diversion or both.

And I understood the situation in Farad. The seesaw struggle for power had been going on between these two for so many years that the Prince by now was in automatic opposition to the wishes of his priesthood. Therein, very possibly, lay the factor that might win Prince Kraa to assist us in the quest.

In a word, I did not have to exert my authority as the Jamad. It was not necessary, for the Prince would convince himself to aid our purpose. By now he was conditioned to turn left, whenever he believed the priests, led by Dhu, wanted him to turn right!

"We await your answer, O Dhu! Is it—can it—be sacrilege to search after something that is not even there? Why should the Timeless Ones forbid such a curious thing?"

Dhu gathered himself together and managed to find something to say.

"Yes, O Prince!" he said. "Because . . . by forbidding Ilionis to exist, the Timeless Ones are telling us not to look for it."

The Prince said nothing. Dhu licked his lips, eyes uncertain; that sounded like pretty bad logic, even to him. He went on, losing momentum visibly.

"And anyway, the Sacred Land is forbidden to all men."

"True," the Prince nodded, with a quiet smile. "But that is a prohibition enacted by the Jamad Jonnath XII of the Silver Dynasty. By his law, we stand guard here in this place forever, so that men shall not enter the Sacred Land. Is it not true, what I say?"

Dhu nodded uncertainly: it was as if he knew what was coming.

"But the law a Jamad makes, another Jamad can rescind. Is that not equally true?"

Dhu nodded miserably and shot me a glance that was a shaft of pure poison.

"But the land is inviolable in ancient custom, and the priesthood invokes the curse of the Timeless Ones upon he who desecrates the sacredness of tradition," he snarled.

"The Jamad is holier than any priest," I observed calmly. "And I too can *curse*."

The hunched little priest paled, for he knew the Power I bore and could guess the strength of my curses!

"Can any action of a crowned Jamad Tengru be sacrilege?" asked the Prince thoughtfully. "I doubt if it can. Since the Jamad is himself the very embodiment of the Law. As well, he is guided by the cumulative wisdom and inspiration of the holy wearers of that Crown who went before him. And is it not written in a thousand scriptures that the Timeless Ones watch over the Jamad and guide his steps? How could the gods lead the Jamad into impiety or sacrilege? The thought is impossible . . . would you not say, priest?"

Dhu wilted. He nodded sullenly, not deigning to meet my smile or the bland, bright gaze of Prince Kraa.

And for the rest of the feast, he sat unmoving, savoring the sour taste of defeat.

And it was thus that I won the aid of the Moon Dragon Prince for the quest.

No cunning or cleverness on my part did the deed. The Prince more or less talked himself into it.

And little Dhu helped, of course, by opposing the whole thing. It is wonderful how the arguments of a hated rival can drive you to follow a course you do not actually want to take!

9. The Road to Ilionis

Two days after the great feast in the Hall of the Moons, we were ready to depart on the final leg of our journey.

Our guide to the site of the Lost City would be none other than Prince Kraa. The old man stoutly refused to permit one of his chieftains to dare the curse of the Timeless Ones. If it should indeed prove an act of sacrilege to guide Outworlders across the borders of the Sacred Land, the Prince was determined that the sin and its punishment should fall upon his head alone. He would not permit another to take the risk.

Kuruk, in turn, was every bit as adamant in refusing to permit his father to undertake the dangerous and difficult journey. He pointed out that Kraa was an old man and that the hazards and perils of the trip might well prove too much for him.

The argument continued at some length and was not finally resolved until Prince Kraa reluctantly agreed to let Lord Kuruk accompany us. The minstrel Huw demanded to be included in the expedition, saying that the court would be intolerably dull in the absence of the Prince and the chieftain and that he had always been curious to discover what lay beyond the forbidden borders.

The moon-faced little minstrel was, it seems, something of a pampered favorite with the old prince. And so it was decided that Huw would ride with us; Kraa observed that while the fat little minstrel would prove of no value in a battle, he could at least entertain us with his songs.

The boy Chaka also would not be left behind. He put up such a loud outcry at the notion of being left out of the first real adventure to come along in years, that the old Prince agreed he should come, if only to restore peace and quiet.

That, at least, was the excuse he gave in public.

Privately the Prince admitted that it was time the youth had a taste of danger and discomfort.

"It is never too early to begin the long task of becoming a man," he said gruffly. "A boy cannot begin too young. Someday, perhaps, he will be Prince in my place; if so, it would be well if he saw something of the world and its perils, if only to learn the wisdom of prudence and caution and the value of courage and daring."

So it was decided: the boy would be my servant. At news of this Chaka was ecstatic. Perhaps he felt rather as a boy might have, back in medieval times, when chosen to serve some noble knight as his squire. Not that I was much of a knight, I fear!

And so the expedition grew and grew; warriors would ride with us to guard our safety and lackeys to serve us, to tend our beasts, and to prepare our meals.

A less agreeable companion in our adventure also announced his intention of traveling the long road to Ilionis with us: the priest Dhu, who stiffly claimed it as a right of his birth. As pontiff of the Timeless Ones in Chun, one of his ceremonial titles was hereditary guardian of the Gates of Yhoom, the mythical underworld of the Martian gods. In the symbolism of the ancient legends Ilionis meant "the gateway" and was popularly believed to represent a mystical bridge between the World Above, where the People dwelt, and the World Below, where the gods dwelt among the spirits of the blessed dead.

So he demanded his right to go along and to protect the holy places from the desecrations of the *F'yagha.*

"I tol' you this was no good," Bolgov growled to the Doctor when he heard of these events. "We'll have the whole damn city stepping on our heels before we get there! How the hell we going to get away with the treasure, with all these bloody Cats along, ready t'cut our throats if we so much as look cross-eyed at one of their heathen idols?"

Keresny soothed his ire with gentle remonstrances, but in private he complained to me about the growth in our ranks. But there was really little I could say or do to discourage the new members of our party from accompanying us, for that would have planted suspicions about our true purpose and motives and inflame superstitious fears of desecration already exacerbated by Dhu's fiery rhetoric.

So they had to come along.

Though how we were going to deal with them, once we reached Ilionis, was beyond me.

I no longer had much doubt that we would find the Lost City: from of old, Farad had been established here to guard the road to holy Ilionis, and the coincidence that this old legend existed in such close proximity to the actual or supposed site of the Lost City, as given in the thought record Keresny had found, was too much to be called a coincidence.

Ilionis was there, all right. Like the leprechaun's pot of gold at the end of the rainbow.

But it yet remained to be seen whether there was any gold in the pot.

Before we departed from Farad, there was an important ceremony to be enacted. This was the swearing of fealty unto the Jamad by the Moon Dragon Prince.

The ceremony was simplicity itself. In the full presence of his assembled lords, nobles, and chieftains, the old Prince knelt, kissed again the dirt before me, and lay his naked sword at my feet.

By this ancient rite he made himself my man and swore his Vow to serve me in all things . . . he and his nation.

But the ceremonial was capable of yet another interpretation too.

But yielding sovereignty to me, he also lay at my feet the responsibility for what we were about to do. As my liege-man, Prince Kraa no longer bore any responsibility for whatever sacrilege or blasphemy our quest might entail.

For my will thus became his law.

And if the gods of Mars were angered at this intrusion upon the Sacred Land, their wrath and vengeance would fall on me and not upon Kraa, my thrall, who was innocent of wrongdoing by his oath of fealty.

It was a handsome bit of "buck-passing," as the Americans might call it.

The Prince's face was bland and innocent as he rose to his feet and received his sword from my hand; but little Dhu glowered sullenly the while.

The political shrewdness of the move had so many ramifications that it kept me amused, just untangling them, while we rode out through the gates of Farad and into the barren waste that stretched across the great Chun plateau to the forbidden borders of the Sacred Land.

All that day we rode on across a rocky wilderness, pausing only twice to relieve nature and to let the beasts rest.

The old Prince rode at the head of our party by my side. He spoke but little, his eyes roving keenly about; he sat ramrod stiff in the saddle. He proved tireless, veteran of a hundred wars that he was, and it was not long before he ceased viewing our quest with unease and forboding and began to enjoy the adventure. His good humor did not sour, nor did his long hours of hard-riding drain his strength or lessen his zest for the expedition.

Behind us the little priest Dhu rode along, grumbling almost continually. No seasoned rider he! A thousand times he complained of the jouncing stride of his *slidar,* of the looseness of his saddle harness, of the burning thirst that tormented him, and of the discomfort of the journey.

Every slightest mishap that occurred, he seized upon to shrilly proclaim an ill omen. Loose shale made one of the beasts lose its footing and stumble, causing an inattentive warrior to take a fall. The man arose unhurt, dusting himself off and grinning shame-facedly. But the hunchback keened like an old woman who had just heard the sobbing cry of the banshee and scents a death in the family.

The Prince harshly bade him hold his tongue or go back to the safety of Farad. Thereafter Dhu made no further lamentations, but he continued to grumble and to chant half-audible prayers to avert the vengeance of the Timeless Ones—under his breath, of course, but just loud enough for us to be aware.

Regardless of his loud-voiced attitude of fatalism, nothing whatever occurred to imperil us or even to slow us down until sundown and the darkening of the world.

Weary from a long day in the saddle, we decided to make camp, eat, and take to our sleeping furs. But a bit of excitement broke the monotony of the venture.

A thundering hiss exploded like a jet of live steam. The *slidars* showed their fangs and bucked widely, eyeballs glistening with naked fear. A drift of innocent-looking yellow sand directly in our path erupted as if a dynamite charge had been set off beneath it.

And out of its hidden lair a sandcat scrambled, roaring for meat and blood!

Ilsa screamed as her *slidar* reared, kicking and squealing in panic terror, throwing her from the saddle. Claws rasping against harsh stone, the scarlet monster hurled itself upon her prone body.

It had all happened so suddenly that even the experienced hunters among our guard of warriors were frozen with shock. I knew that the terrible predators prowled the highlands of the plateau regions—I had even heard they made their dens in pits and crevices, which they somehow roofed over with sand, not unlike Earth's humbler little predators, the trapdoor spiders. But even I was not prepared for this emergency.

The thing was nine feet of slithering scarlet ferocity, armed with monstrous claws that could gut a full-grown *slidar* at a single slash, and it was virtually unkillable, at least with the bronze or copper spears with which our guards went armed.

The sandcat looks very much like a sort of crimson tiger, but it is really not a feline or even a mammal, but a reptile, cold-blooded, rapacious, and clad in tough horny scales. This mailed hide is impervious to even the deadly blowdarts, and bronze-bladed weapons lack the hardness of point to pierce the sandcat in a vital organ. An iron spearhead, or better yet, one of steel, would have made sandcat-hunting far easier than it is; but iron, of course, is the rarest of metals on this ancient world.

In the milling chaos, fighting to gain control of our fear-maddened steeds, we could not even get at the sandcat with what weapons we did have.

Ilsa shrieked again. Through a momentary chink in the mass of churning limbs and whirling bodies, I saw the crimson horror ripping and tearing at Ilsa's fallen steed. Another flying glimpse, and I saw she lay pinned under the *slidar*.

Beside me at that moment, Bolgov clung to his wildly bucking mount. I saw the pistol butt in its holster at his thigh. In the next split second I was off my *slidar*—half-falling and half-jumping clear of the saddle.

I fell to one knee. Scrambled up, lunging through the whirling dust to where Bolgov clung with both arms to the neck of his beast. Then I snatched the weapon from his holster and staggered through a sudden opening in the crowd of surging beasts and yelling men.

Dropping to one knee, I steadied the gun against my forearm and fired point-blank at the scarlet horror. It was a .34V General Electric lasergun. A pencil of brilliant red light drew a line of sparkling fire between the muzzle and the cat. The gloom lit around us with a ruddy glare.

The sandcat squalled! Bit furiously at its seared shoulder, where the lance of intolerable fire had blackened the glistening, scaly hide. I fired again—aiming at the throat—missed, and it saw me. Somehow that cold reptilian intelligence guessed that it was I who had caused it the hurt. It left the mangled hulk of the *slidar* and threw itself at me so swift it was only a red blur in the dimness.

I fired the lasergun again, but this time without even taking aim, letting pure instinct serve. Again the needle of ruby fire licked out, lighting the gloom with its weird, lambent glow. Then something about the weight and speed of a turbotrain slammed into me and knocked me flying. I crashed head first into solid rock and slid away from everything for a time.

I awoke from darkness slowly, my skull cracking open in the throes of a headache of epic proportions. There was a strange odor heavy in my nostrils. I lay there, blinking fuzzily at blackness, wondering vaguely what it was that I was smelling.

Then everything came back to me at once—the sandcat —*Ilsa!* And I half-sprang up from the rocky ground where I had been sprawling. And settled back with a groan, gritting my teeth as bright agony ripped through my brain. Tenderly, I raised one hand to my throbbing brow: it came away wet and sticky.

A tall shape stooped over me. I could make out a heavy, grim face and a russet furcap, gray at the temples.

"Kuruk?"

"Lord! Are you hurt—?"

"The cat?"

He laughed a bit shakily and said, "Dead, Lord. *Broiled to death*, like a gobbet on the griddle!"

Then it was that I recognized the heavy odor that lay thick in the air about us. It was the unmistakable aroma of broiled meat.

Kuruk helped me to rise and wet a cloth from his waxhide canteen to bathe my brow. Men stood laughing and talking around the immense corpse of the sandcat. They parted to let me limp through, and there it was, stone dead, its whole head a ragged, crisped mass of steaming meat.

By sheer luck the laserbeam had caught it in the eye, perhaps, or square in its open mouth, between fanged and gaping jaws. The fiery needle had pierced to its brain, cooked it alive, exploding the sandcat's head like a rotten apple.

Ilsa was white and shaken, but unharmed, save for a bruise or two and a few scratches. I grinned at her through the gloom and warmed at her tremulous, answering smile.

Prince Kraa was jubilant and thrilled: he had never seen one of the *F'yagha* energy weapons in action before, it seemed. From the amazed faces of the warriors and the awe in their voices, it would seem they regarded my accidental slaying of the charging sandcat as something in the nature of a miracle. I grinned wryly, aware that my reputation had just gone up another notch in their estimate.

Hands trembling a bit with the nervous reaction from the flurry of excitement, Dr. Keresny hauled out the medikit and treated my scalp wound with something cool and slick and sulfur smelling. He snapped a suction bandage in place and pronounced me fit for duty.

We mounted and rode forward for a time, even though the darkness was all but impenetrable by now. Sandcats are loners and tolerate the presence of another of the species but briefly once a year, during the rutting season; but there must be more of the scarlet horrors on this part of the plateau, and the stench of cooked meat would draw them like flies before the corpse was cold. And I did not feel up to facing five more sandcats, even with a lasergun in my hands.

Eventually we found a cozy nook, a bowl-shaped hollow ringed with ridged hills. It was too damn dark to tell whether it was another of the omnipresent craters or a natural formation, but it hardly mattered, and we were ravenous for food and aching for sleep. We ate swiftly and without words, under the winter-sharp glitter of the many-colored stars, and crept away to sleep. The Moon Dragon warriors curled up in those heavy sacks of *orthava* fleece they call "sleeping furs," but we Earthside types chose thermal tents and inflatable mattresses.

My head was troubling me again, so I took a pill and slid off over the edge of sleep. The last thing I heard before sleep claimed me was the squeak of boots crunching in sand grit as the guards of the first watch paced slowly about the perimeter of our rock bowl.

But I awoke to startled yells!

I had been so worn out the night before that I had not even bothered to take off my thermal suit but had slept in it. Hence, I was on my feet and fumbling to unseam the tent at the first yell and a moment later stood blinking in the sun's glare, still not quite fully awake and a bit groggy from the sedative.

I saw at first glance what had aroused the startled outcries. I don't know just what I had expected—maybe another sandcat, out for an early-morning prowl—but this was quite a different breed of intruder.

It stood about four meters high and glared down at us from sightless eyes, massive arms folded upon its breast. I stood, panting, waiting for my racing heart to slow down a little, looking back at it.

A hand was on my arm. I turned; Ilsa, face flushed from sleep, hair a warm odor on the keen dawn air, eyes filled with marvel.

"What on earth . . . !"

I forced a laugh. "Mars, rather! Another no-trespassing sign, like the one back in Hareton Rill; but a trifle more artistic this time."

The Doctor was at our side now, shivering in the cold as he seamed up his thermal suit and turned up the heating element. His wondering gaze studied the tall black thing with delight.

"*Very* ancient work," he mused half-aloud. "From the style, at least; but look at the surface condition of the stone. Smooth and slick as glass . . . It should be weathered, pitted, scarred . . . Could it be onyx? Hardly likely! Diorite?"

Just beyond the sloping entryway that led into the rock bowl (which, I now saw, clearly *was* an impact crater), stood a tall, glassy pillar of jet-black stone, whose upper half was beautifully sculptured into the likeness of a frowning Martian giant: one of the *ushongti,* the guardian genii of legend, with the traditional three-horned brow, elongated earlobes, and hideous tusks hooked down over its pendulous lower lip. We had passed it in the darkness without seeing it last night, when we rode down into the crater to make camp. Some sleepy guard, trudging a weary circuit around the camp this morning, must have almost walked into the glaring stone monster before he noticed it. I grinned at the picture: I would have let out a yell myself, had I come upon the thing unaware!

Keresny clambered up the steep slope of the ringwall to its crest and summoned us excitedly.

"Look! Look!" he crowed, face agleam with the scientist's exultation at a discovery. We followed his trembling, pointing finger and looked.

Straight as a die, from the edge of the crater to the horizon, a fantastic double row of stone *ushongti* marched into the distance. There must have been ten thousand of the sculptured black diorite monoliths!

"Look at the lane between the rows," Ilsa cried. "It's as smooth as a road! Not a crater or a crevice or even a fallen boulder!"

An unholy glee blazed in Keresny's eyes.

"It *is* a road, my dear. *The road to Ilionis!*"

I said nothing. But I had a horrible feeling he was right.

10. The Avenue of Monoliths

Our entourage did not at all care for the silent stone colossusses that brooded down upon us as we rode between them all that day. The glower of those scowling eyes, those frowning faces of slick black stone, cast a pall over our spirits. Kraa rode at my side as before, but now his gaunt face was somber and his eyes were sad and thoughtful, as if dwelling upon grim inward visions. Even the ugly little priest had neither the energy nor the spite to grumble and complain today; he too rode silently, lost in his own thoughts, an indefinable fear stamped on his froglike features.

Nor did I feel particularly gleeful, either. I was cursedly stiff and sore from the tumble I had taken last evening, when the sandcat had run amok and charged into me, and a rare mood of black depression had clamped down upon my spirits. This statue-lined boulevard obviously led somewhere. Nobody was going to go to all the expense and labor of carving, transporting, and erecting all these thousands of tons of stone to make a double row pointing *nowhere.* And the only place they could lead to was the Lost City itself.

Which meant that before too many days were past, I would be up against a problem I had not as yet wrestled with. For a long time I had been kidding myself. For too long I had postponed even thinking about the thing. Now it seemed time was running out. Before very much longer, I would have to come to a decision. I would have to decide just exactly what I was going to do once we got to Ilionis and found its age-old treasure.

Was I going to fulfill my promise and help Keresny and Bolgov loot the ancient city of its precious wealth? True, I had never actually promised to do so in so many words; I had said that I would use my influence with the natives to help them get to the Lost City. I had said nothing about helping them rob the holy place of its treasure.

But even though I had not explicitly committed myself on the point, we had a tacit understanding, the Doctor and I. And I would have to exert my influence one way or another: either by commanding the Moon Dragon warriors to carry the plunder out of the Lost City to our skimmer, or by refusing to bend them to my command.

This, of course, would make it impossible to plunder Ilionis. Keresny and Bolgov could hardly transport the treasure alone and unaided. And unless I interposed my authority to protect them, I knew Prince Kraa and his people would not stand calmly by and let the ancient vaults be ransacked by the Earthmen. They would either seize or slay the *F'yagha,* and most likely it would be the latter. Especially since the viper-eyed little pontiff would doubtless be foaming at the mouth with rage at the sacrilege.

Ilsa I would protect at any cost, of course. And I could hardly see myself standing by idly while the enraged Moon Dragon warriors killed her grandfather and Bolgov. As for Bolgov—well, I cared nothing for him, of course, and the feeling was mutual. On the other hand, while I disliked the surly, black-bearded Ukranian, he hadn't actually done anything against me, except to call me a dirty name or two and take a poke at me once. I'm as squeamish as the next citizen, and I don't think I could just stand there and watch the poor bastard being butchered without trying to help him.

As for the Doctor, he had never done anything against me at all. I rather liked the old fellow in a mild way. He had been unfailingly polite and even friendly toward me; and without his kindness I would still be back in Venice, swilling down cheap brandy in the arcade by the cathedral of San Pietro. Of course, he had brought me here for his own reasons, not mine; and those reasons were completely selfish. But did it really matter why he had done it? Didn't I owe him something for bringing me back to the world I loved?

In any event, he was an old man, and Ilsa loved him. I would have to protect him—yes, and even Bolgov, I suppose—against the Martian warriors.

But I didn't have to lend them any help in robbing the treasure vaults of Ilionis!

I could just refuse to do anything and refuse to ask of Prince Kraa's warriors that which they would not willingly do. Oh, Keresny would rant and rave, surely; maybe even Bolgov would bluster and wave his gun around. But in the end, there wouldn't be much they could do about it.

Yes, that was probably the wisest course to follow.

One thing was certain. I could not, and would not, jeopardize my relationship with the Prince of Farad by forcing him to command his men to help the Hated Ones rob ancient and holy Ilionis of its fabled treasure. That would be a vile way to repay Prince Kraa for his hospitality and his friendship.

Oh, I was fairly certain that the Prince would obey me if I were foolish and cruel enough to command him, as his Jamad. But were I to make him break his own laws and violate his own traditions to that extent, I would lose his friendship forever. He would cast his vow of fealty back into my teeth; the gates of Farad would close in my face forever; and never, while the world lasts, would the legions of the Moon Dragon nation ride to war against the Earthmen under my banner.

Yes, I was willing to break the spirit, if not the letter, of my promise to Dr. Keresny, rather than cripple my forces in the coming holy war and alienate the Moon Dragon Prince and his heirs for all time.

And it passed through my mind right then that I would be wise to keep a wary eye on Bolgov during the next few days. For once I made it plain that I would not help them get the treasure out, it was not at all impossible that Bolgov would do something crazy, like putting that gun to my head to make the Martians carry out the plunder, at peril of the life of their Jamad.

No, I'd better keep an eye peeled for the big Ukranian; he was a rough, unscrupulous type, and he would stop at little to get what he wanted. Maybe there was some way I could get the gun away from him . . . I would have to mull the problem over and see what I could come up with. I put the whole question out of my mind for the moment, promising to give it some further thought later on, when it became relevant.

I would to God I had not set the problem aside at that time! If only I had seized the thought the moment it occurred to me! If only I had turned my beast to one side— had ridden back to Bolgov's place in the procession—and had simply snatched the gun away from him then and there!

Busied each with our different thoughts, we galloped on down the avenue of black monoliths under the far, pale fire disc of the distant sun.

The Doctor had been keeping mental count of the number of stone *ushongti* that lined the way to Ilionis for the eventual book or article or monograph he would refine from his experiences, but after counting five thousand of the glaring diorite images, he gave it up. I think the gloom and apprehension that haunted the rest of us as we rode along, hour by hour, under the ominous frown of the stone genii, got to him eventually and dampened even his keen excitement. For the shadow of foreboding seemed to darken his fine eyes and lend his features a worn and weary aspect.

As for big Kuruk, the grizzled veteran was no less susceptible to the mood of apprehension that gripped us all; but he rode at my back, faithful and watchful as some great dog. I think it was enough for the grim-faced chieftain that his Prince and his Jamad were there to guard and to worry over. I looked back once, feeling his eyes on me, and smiled to see him. He sat his saddle easily, unwearyingly, one hand at the pommel of his sword, his narrow eyes prowling to all sides watchfully, ever alert for the chance of danger.

Faithful, simple, brave Kuruk! Staunch comrade in battle, unyielding and untiring friend! I knew his kind of manhood, for my legions had been filled with many such —but never with enough. The sort of man who gave you his whole heart and strength and loyalty when he swore his oath to you: and never retracted it, even to the death.

Give me a thousand Kuruks and I could have conquered all of Mars years ago. No; give me only one hundred and I could make a damn good try!

As for Chaka, the boy was the only one whose bright eyes were undimmed by the grim row of glowering giants. He rode with his shoulders back, his eyes alive and eager in his bright face, afire with youthful excitement and hungry to obey any whim of mine. I grinned at his clear eyes and fiery zest. He would follow his grandfather to the dais of Farad—among the Martian princes, inheritance is through the female line, and it would be the son of Prince Kraa's widowed daughter who would inherit the rule of Farad, not his own son, Kuruk. And he would make a strong Prince and a good one, I knew.

We had been riding for some hours now. I could not rid myself of a feeling of uneasiness, a prickling sensation at the back of my neck, as if my nape hairs had stiffened, sensing the touch of unseen eyes, watching, watching . . .

An aura of ancient mystery brooded over this bleak land like a hovering shadow. There was strangeness here, and there was also that which was more than merely strange: a dim premonition of *otherness* lurked at the far borders of comprehension.

There was the silence, for one thing. Sound carries

poorly in the thin air of Mars, but surely such taut, breath-less silence as hung about us here was no natural thing. Why did the pads of our mounts fall dully on the harsh, gritty stone? Why did it seem that the creak of saddle leather, the jingle of our accouterments, the clash of weap-ons, the rustling of our cloaks—all sounded dim and far-off, as if oddly *muffled?*

And why did a party of thirty warriors and personages ride in such somber and unspeaking silence? Even lazy, laughing Huw no longer hummed a tuneless song under his breath—no longer strummed a jaunty, jangling tune on his many-stringed *odyar*—but rode glumly, slumped brooding in the saddle, his bland grin and cheerful eyes shadowed as if by some nameless foreboding.

And there was the Road itself. All about to either side the barren, rocky tableland stretched away, cleft by ten thousand cracks and crevices, riddled with volcanic fu-maroles and pockmarked by the innumerable impact craters, small and large, that peppered the surface of the planet from pole to pole. *But the Road ran ever on!* And for all of its die-straight length visible to us, it was un-blemished.

As if some unseen and omnipresent force shielded the stony way from even the hurtling meteorites of heaven and preserved it unchangingly in the very teeth of time . . .

Strange as it was, this was to prove but the least, and the first, of many mysteries!

We made early camp that day, and we chose for our camping site the Road itself, for all that we no longer cared to meet the carved glower of the frowning colossusses.

But we somehow knew, all of us, that whatever mon-strous predators might prowl this land by night, here we would be safe from attack and alarm. And how we knew this thing we could not say, but neither did we question it.

Perhaps the long day of riding had wearied us and sapped our spirits; or mayhap it was the shadowy gloom that brooded over this desolate and terrible land where naught but we moved or lived under the carved glare of the monolith monsters; but whatever the reason, our hearts did not lift with the coming of darkness. The white glare of the campfire (fed by those same chemicals which had blazed on the hearths and in the bronze cressets of the Hall of the Moons) did not warm us. Even a bellyful of hot meat did not lift our mood of ominous oppression. Neither did the cold red wine of Farad bring joy to our hearts. We ate in silence and drank without words and went to our furs, unspeaking.

I sought out Huw. The fat minstrel sprawled lazily, pillowed on his saddle, rubbing the soreness from aching leg muscles, looking thoughtfully up at the stars. Like strewn gems they were, and they blazed fiercely on the black velvet of the sky. At my approach he would have risen, but I gestured to him to remain where he was, as I sat wearily on heaped saddlebags. He eyed me somberly.

"You feel it too, Lord?"

My voice was heavy. "Yes. Like a cold black pall laid upon my heart. What is it, Huw—you, a minstrel, are a master of the lore—what is it haunts us?"

He scratched his ear and rubbed a big hand slowly over his fat jowls. "Magic, I suppose . . . The sagas tell that the Ancients had some weird power to oppress the hearts of men with dark sadness and with the echo of unheard warnings. Oft in the old tales the holy places were thus guarded from impieties . . . Oh, 'tis mad enough, I wager, this babble of sorceries and spells. Yet I do feel it, nonetheless, like a cold hand upon the roots of my soul . . ."

I frowned thoughtfully. *Subsonics?* Could it be something as simple, as mundane, as merely a projection of sound waves? Could the Ancients have known that sound waves, projected at certain intensities and wavelengths, can make people edgy, nervous, tense, depressed—or, conversely, excited and happy?

Could that be the purpose for this meaningless row of stone colossusses that marched off across the world? Did concealed mechanisms within their towering pillars project or conduct an omnipresent, mood-dampening vibration— sound pitched too low for the ear to hear, sound sensed in the very blood and bone?

"They were a great folk, Lord, eh, with strange mastery

of unknown forces," Huw muttered, as if receptive to the very thoughts that passed through my brain. " 'Twould be cleverness itself—would it not?—to drive away the unwanted visitor, the intruder into this land, by some strange witch art that preys on his taut nerve until it breaks, and he flees, mad with a fear he cannot even name? For, look you, Lord, the beasts themselves sense it!"

That was true enough, I knew. All day, ever since we had ridden between the first pair of scowling stone genii, the *slidars* had been restive, snappish, and unruly beyond even the wont of their temperamental kind. And with evening we had been forced to bed them down outside of the Avenue of Monoliths, if they were not to panic and break into flight.

Some of the rude, superstitious warriors were already murmuring of curses and ghosts and of the shadow of some ancient and malignant evil that haunted all this land . . . But could it be (I stared up, wondering, at the demon-shaped black pillars, where they loomed against the stars) that those tall, standing stones were nothing more weird or wondrous than—*antennae?*

I clapped Huw on the shoulder and rose stiffly to seek my own sleeping furs and the privacy of my thoughts. But the weariness of the long, shadow-haunted day overcame me instead, and I slept. But it was a fitful and an uneasy sleep, made terrible by dreams wherein dim enormous things swayed and moved closer—*closer*—and from whose never-seen but momentarily-to-be-revealed faces I awoke shuddering, time and again, through the long, cold watches of the uneasy night.

The sun was a pale disc of cool gray fire part-way up the dome of the sky when I awoke from broken dreams of spectral terror. Perhaps it was the bitter coldness of the air or the bleak deadness of this accursed and barren, rocky land, but even the dawning of the day star did little to lift our spirits.

We broke our fast and saddled up our mounts, Keresny aligning his Mars compass and checking his maps. But this was mere scholarly absentness or thoroughness, for the

Road fell before us like an outstretched and pointing arm, marking the very direction in which we must travel.

All that second day we moved on toward Ilionis. None of us doubted that it would be there, though none of us could have guessed the strange miracle we should find.

The *slidars* grew ever more unruly and bad tempered, rearing at a shadow, throwing many a warrior, and turning on more than one rider to snap glistening fangs at knee or thigh. Indeed, toward midday one of the gaunt red beasts went mad and turned on another with slashing teeth, in a spitting tangle of threshing limbs. In the end both beasts had to be slain.

We, ourselves, suffered ever more keenly from the unseen assault. Nerves stretched tight to the breaking point, and suddenly quarrels—even stormy bursts of hysteria and weeping—exploded without reason. We ate little and drank less, the meat and wine somehow tasteless in our mouths.

More and more the men muttered of phantoms and of terrible and ancient curses. Eyes rolled from side to side restlessly, showing the whites, and many a stout warrior's calloused hand surreptitiously fondled an amulet or periapt or charm; and many the hardened fighting man who rode forward, mumbling imprecations or litanies to half the hundred gods of Mars, frightened almost to the naked edge of panic by—*nothing!*

I will not even try to guess how much longer we could have endured this siege of shadows.

But—suddenly and without the slightest warning—it was over!

The land before us had been obscured by a strange haze that had blurred our vision. In the weird mixture of lethargy and tension wherein we were all enveloped, it had not occurred to us to wonder at this: for on water-poor Mars, mists or fog or clouds of any kind are never found.

But in the turning of one instant of time the hazy blur vanished; and in that same instant the uneasiness and fear that had held us under its spell also ended.

It was as if we had ridden beyond the zone of some force and were at last in the clear again.

Which may, in fact, have been the case.
But we reined to a sudden halt, gaping.
And there before us lay . . . *Ilionis!*
We stared for a long time, without words.

O, it was old, that city; old and dead. Ages beyond the numbering of man had trampled it down into the dust. The once-proud walls lay fallen in huge sections. The houses and mansions were empty, gutted—black windows leering like the eye sockets of hollow skulls. Sand had drifted, grain by grain, into the silent streets, until they were carpeted with dust.

All of red marble was lost and ruined Ilionis, and the centuries had cracked and pitted and splintered that dead stone to crumbling ruins. The broken towers and fallen rubble lay ghostly before us in the dim light of the dying day, and it well may be that no living eyes had looked on Ilionis for millions of years, before our coming.

"A rose-red city, half as old as time . . ."

The line from the old poem rose unbidden from my memory. The poet had set down those immortal words to Petra, but this dim red city was older far by a thousand ages.

Once it had been king city of a mighty empire and the center of the ancient faith; *Gateway to the Gods,* the old epics name it. Now it was dead, empty, deserted, only a dim ghost of its vanished splendor lingered under the hurtling moons.

Somber, unspeaking, we rode down in the twilight to the walls of Ilionis.

And the long quest was ended. We thought.

We could not guess that an even stranger quest had now begun!

11. Gateway to the Gods

The gate pylons of Ilionis still stood, unshivered by time.
Two by two we rode between them into what once had
been a broad and splendid boulevard. But the centuries,
like vandals, had been here before us, and paving stones
were split and cracked and tilted, some half-drowned in
remorseless yellow dust-fine sand. Beside me Ilsa shud-
dered, and her face was sad and wan.

"How terribly sad," she whispered. "All that majesty
and greatness . . . gone."

I nodded. "Time has a way with cities," I said. "It does
not really approve of anything less permanent than moun-
tains, I suppose. Or stars. Do you know your Frost at all?"

"Who?"

"American poet, last century. He sensed all this somehow, this enmity the Eternal holds for the trumpery monuments of man. And summed up half a chapter of philoso-
phy or something into one line . . ."

Her face was lovely in the cold light.

"I know; I recall it now. 'Something there is that does
not love a wall.' "

I nodded. "It's as if he had seen Ilionis . . ."

We rode carefully down the ruined street. Darkness was
gathering swiftly, drawing its black cloak across the sky.
The unnatural mood of apprehension, through which we
had ridden for so long, had ended when we passed beyond
the last pair of stone giants. But the awesome wreckage
about us, dim with hoary antiquity, lonely beneath the
glitter of cold stars, was somber and grim. The desolation—the utter silence—was somehow dreadful.

We camped for the night within the shelter of crumbling
walls. Once, long ago this broken shell had been a superb

114

palace or a temple. Now it was a tomb, enshrining the dead dreams of the forgotten hands that had raised these walls to some unknown purpose ages ago.

There was disappointment written in Keresny's face. He peered about, shining his Bronston lamp on mounded rubble, worn and fallen columns, heavily carved doorways leading nowhere.

"Even the inscriptions are too worn to be legible," he said. "Somehow, I had expected more than this. I don't know just what. Not an inhabited city, like Farad, but . . . *something.*"

I understood his mood, I think, and the disappointment that lurked behind his inarticulate words. For Ilionis was not only dead: the very mood and spirit of the ruin was extinct. Not even ghosts would linger amid this awful desolation. It was like the wreckage of man's hopes—the ruins of a forgotten dream.

At least we slept soundly that night, and no shadowy terrors haunted our slumber. The *slidars* too rested easy, recovering their normal placidity.

The next day we organized things with Prince Kraa's aid. The ruin was quartered off, and a party of Moon Dragon warriors were assigned to search each sector of the Lost City under the guidance of an Earthman.

We were alert to note significant structures, major monuments, or undamaged inscriptions of importance. Most of that day was spent combing the rubble, exploring half-ruined buildings, strolling through empty streets. In late afternoon we gathered again in our temporary camp to compare notes. Little enough of any value had we found; Ilsa's party had located some inscriptions which remained legible after aeons; my group had found a major shrine which still stood; and Bolgov had scouted a tremendous edifice toward the heart of the dead metropolis that bore the semblance of a main temple.

But the disappointment was written deep in the Doctor's weary face as he studied the depth pictures he had taken.

"The inscriptions are either in one of the Lost Tongues or are merely commemorative," he sighed, setting them aside.

"What of my shrine?" I asked. He shrugged dispiritedly.

"The sepulchers are marked with the royal cartouches," he replied. "And the wall inscriptions are nothing more than antique forms of the familiar *huakan,* tablets raised to the memory of the ancestors of the buried kings. Oh, doubtless of great historical importance, of course. But somehow I had expected more . . ."

It was Bolgov, in his blunt way, who touched on the central question.

"Where is the *treasure* supposed to be, damnit!"

"That's just it, Konstantin," the Doctor said sadly. "We don't know just where it is; here, somewhere, but . . . *where?*"

"But Grandfather, what about the thought record? Didn't it describe a definite site?"

"No, my dear, it did not. I had thought the treasure vault would be very conspicuous, very clearly marked. Some building so huge as to dominate the rest of the structures in the city, calling attention to itself. But it would seem that I have been mistaken," he said with something very like despair in his voice.

Bolgov began to redden.

"You mean we come all this way for *nothing?*" he demanded. "Jus' some lousy inscriptions and these damn ruins?"

"It is still too soon to tell for certain, Konstantin," the Doctor argued faintly. "Perhaps the treasure is better hidden than I had conjectured . . ."

"What about those kings' tombs?" he asked greedily. "Maybe they got gold and gems buried with 'em; 's worth a try!"

"I doubt if our host would permit the royal sepulchers to be opened," I warned. "We are here on sufferance and had best not appear to be treasure hunters."

Konstantin started to blurt out some angry response, but Keresny silenced him. "The burial customs of the Ancients are well known," he said. "The old kings were cremated, and nothing was ever buried with them except for a ceremonial copy of the Book of Kings."

"There's still that major temple," I pointed out. "The one Bolgov's party scouted out. He said it was just too big to explore thoroughly."

"Yes, there is that," Keresny mused, rubbing his brows thoughtfully. "Tomorrow we'll have a look at it . . ."

The following day we ventured deep into the center of the Lost City to examine the central structure. It certainly dominated the surrounding ruins, built upon a height as it was; and it was the largest edifice still standing.

Once it had been a cruciform temple, crowned with the traditional five domes, the arms of the ground floor oriented to the cardinal points of the compass. Time had brought its heaviest siege artillery to bear against it, however, and two of the wings were collapsed into stone heaps. But the central nave, the holy of holies, and the west and north wings still held up under the battery of the centuries.

Like most of the other ancient temples on Mars, the gates were guarded by stone sphinxes depicting those weird, insectlike, imaginary beasts. We entered the hall between them, up a flight of shallow steps worn by the tread of countless generations of worshipers. The gloomy vastnesses of the remaining temple stretched off in all directions, loud with echoes and dim with drifted dust.

There were endless vestibules and antechambers to explore, but nothing of any particular significance was found in any of them. More inscriptions, both in the unknown tongue and in the more familiar glyphs we could read. Bits of broken pottery, chipped and worthless votive figures, a few pieces of worn but good statuary, a few scraps of withered parchment—all that the remorseless passage of the years had left of ancient books and old tapestries. That was about it.

The day was exhausted in a systematic exploration of the two wings that time had left still standing. Here the resident priests had been housed, but nothing of worth was found in the endless succession of identical cells and cubicles. Keresny, armed with the Bronston lamps, led an exploring party into the lower levels, but most of the passageways had collapsed and were hopelessly blocked with wreckage. And those few portions which could be penetrated disclosed nothing of any particular interest.

That left only the central nave itself. This consisted of the high altar and the holy of holies behind it, which was a huge stone-walled chamber. Aeons ago, when Ilionis had been a living city and this great temple had been odorous with the drifting clouds of incense, bright with votive lamps, and loud with the chanting chorus of priests and worshipers, the yawning portal of the innermost *sanctum sanctorum* had probably been hidden from impious, prying eyes by a huge curtain. If so, the centuries had left nothing of it, and the vast door yawned blackly vacant.

The Doctor had left the *sanctum* for last, because he knew there was little likelihood of our finding anything there. In this particular way the ancient Martian religion was like that of the Jewish kingdom of Earth's own antiquity: the holy of holies was considered the residence of the Divinity. And it was always left empty, save for a copy of the scriptures, which lay on a low pedestal.

We broke for an early meal. While the warriors—who had camped beyond the portals of the temple, reluctant to intrude into the holy place—tended to the *slidars,* the rest of our party sat about on fallen ceiling blocks or rived columns and dined in silence.

Stars glittered with watchful eyes through open places in the domed roof far overhead. The sharp glare of the Bronston lamps painted huge velvet shadows over the walls—shadows that hunched and loomed monstrously as we moved about.

As a gesture of bravado, Prince Kraa and Kuruk and the boy Chaka ate with us, although I knew the Prince, at least, would have preferred to eat out in the open under the gem-strewn skies, rather than in the precincts of the great temple. The dwarfed priest Dhu sat huddled, refusing to profane the altar nave by eating, and mumbled prayers to avert the vengeance of his gods.

In a low voice, so as not to disturb the others, Keresny and I conversed.

"By all rights, the treasure *ought* to have been in the catacombs beneath the nave," he muttered. "Ilionis was a holy city, you know, and the center of yearly world-wide pilgrimages. Votive offerings of jewels and artworks and precious metals must have poured into the hands of the priesthood, for this was the greatest and most sacred of all temples of ancient Mars known to us. The kings of the distant cities would have sent rich gifts in return for the prophecies of the resident oracles; the ill would have journeyed here to be cured by the *arghatha*, the 'healing-priests,' and once their miraculous cures had been effected, would have left as tributes replicas of their various afflicted or injured organs or whatever, worked in gold and silver and Martium. But where is it all?"

"We don't know just when—or why, for that matter—Ilionis became deserted. It's just a speculation, but suppose it was looted in war? The treasure would have been carried off by the victors."

He shook his head. "No, it was not war, my boy. War leaves signs. None of the buildings we have thus far seen bore exterior damage; the walls and gates of the city are fallen, but I saw no signs of siege engines having caused their fall. None of the shrines or frescoes or inscriptions or votive figures have been desecrated or defaced. I believe that Ilionis just died, dwindled away over the ages, as its empire fell into decay. The race has been dying out over millions of years, you know . . . The birthrate has steadily fallen for as long as we have records."

I chewed on the problem for a while in silence.

"You know, it's odd," he said after a time. "We *have* found votive figures and offerings in the outer chambers, but they were humble things—ceramic, worked stone. Perhaps this temple was considered so very holy that to pay offerings or tribute in precious gems or noble metals was construed as blatant bribery and, for that reason, prohibited . . ."

"Well, I suppose that could be so," I said, a trifle dubiously. "But in that case, what the hell did your thought record mean when it said that the greatest treasure of the Ancients was preserved here?"

"I cannot say," he confessed. "What other kinds of treasure are there but—*treasure?*"

"A trove of ancient documents, maybe? A lost library of ancient literature or historical records?"

"Yes, you could call that treasure, I suppose. But even so, where is it all? We found a few moldering scraps of old books, but a cursory examination showed them to be fragments of the usual liturgical and prophetic literature, nothing we did not already possess. No, we have yet to find the place of the treasure."

"A secret chamber then," I suggested.

"Something like that, I suppose. Tomorrow, when the light is better, we shall have to start taking measurements and drawing up a map of the temple ruins. It's just possible that, by comparing the thickness of the walls, we might detect the existence of a hidden room of some kind. We shall have to—"

He started and broke off suddenly as someone yelled.

We jumped to our feet and looked around.

Bolgov appeared suddenly in the entrance of the holy of holies, his face a mask of wild amazement in the harsh glare of the lamps. I had not realized he had finished eating and had strolled off to do a bit of exploring on his own. Now he gestured excitedly, beckoning us to him.

"What is it, Konstantin?" Keresny called. "What have you discovered?"

"Not the treasure, curse th' luck!" the burly Russian growled. "But the damndest thing you ever saw, just the same. C'mere, all of you!"

We took up the Bronston lamps and ascended the steps to the altar and went around the huge, empty stone table where the offerings had been laid before the Timeless Ones, and joined him at the mouth of the great stone room.

I flashed my light around and saw what we had all known we would find, just emptiness and blank walls of stone, devoid even of frescoes or inscriptions.

"Not up there," Bolgov growled impatiently, a suppressed excitement trembling in his voice. *"Look at the floor of the room."*

We directed our lights downward. From where we stood, clustered on the threshold, the floor fell away, forming a vast pit of blackness. The pit stretched from wall to wall, and we could see clearly that this room was no room at all, but the roofed-over top of a tremendous shaft that fell away to unguessable depths beneath the plateau.

Dr. Keresny gasped an exclamation, the light trembling in his shaking hands as he moved the lamp about, exploring the black abyss that yawned before us. And I knew what thought was in his mind: *this* was the anomaly he had expected; for no other temple across the planet contained such an enigma as this mighty pit. And the purpose for which the Ancients had constructed it remained a mystery.

But down there somewhere must be the treasure for which we had come so far and endured so many hazards and discomforts!

To Keresny, I knew, the abyss represented a major archaeological riddle and one he was eager to solve. But my mind was on other matters. For as an engineering feat, the pit represented an astounding accomplishment. I flashed my lamp from side to side of the shaft, marveling. The sheer *size* of the shaft was what made it so fantastic: from wall to wall, it must have measured half a kilometer, perhaps a bit more. And it fell to a depth so great that the light of our Bronston lamps could not discover the bottom.

This central portion of the cruciform temple was built on the solid bedrock of the plateau. The amount of solid stone the tunnel displaced must have been in the millions of tons. Which made the labor of constructing so great a pit one of the greatest engineering feats of all recorded history: you could have constructed a *hundred* pyramids the size of the Great Pyramid of Cheops just from the stone dug out to hollow the shaft! As a work of human labor, it represented the toil of thousands for many generations, perhaps many centuries. The mind was stunned at the enormity of the project. But one question towered above all—

Why!

Why this vast pit, cut from solid rock, descending many kilometers into the core of the planet! That was the real mystery: not *how* it had been done but—*why?*

"*Look*—the far wall!"

I followed the path of the light trembling in Keresny's hands; and there, sloping down the far side of the shaft was a stone stair, cut from the rock itself, a great stair that led down—down—down—

To—*what?*

A hand clamped my arm. Kuruk stood beside me, his heavy face a mask of wondering awe.

"Lord . . . Lord!" he whispered, hoarsely. "The old legends—do you not remember? And the name of the city itself!"

I looked at him dumbly: *Ilionis* was the name of the Lost City in the Tongue; but the Tongue was merely the form to which the language of the Ancients had evolved by the present age. And in the original Old Tongue the name was—

"Ilionis . . . *ylon-ath*," Keresny whispered wonderingly. "*Ylon-ath* means 'Gateway to the Gods' . . ."

"What of it?" I asked, shaken by premonitions of the great wonder yet to come. "It's a common enough name, why, back on Earth, *Babylon* means 'Gateway to the Gods' too . . . And like Babylon, Ilionis was a sacred city, the center of a great religion. It's just a coincidence!"

"But the legends, Lord," Kuruk cried. "Of the Timeless Ones who rule over the dead in their dim Underworld of . . . of Yhoom!"

We stared down at the mighty pit that sank, perhaps, to the very bottom of the world itself; and that was lined with the broad stone stair that led down and down . . . to whatever hidden realm of unguessable mystery lay at the secret core of the very planet.

Staring down and then at one another, our faces lit with dawning amazement, our eyes filled with wide surmise . . . we knew. Knew the truth of it all at last.

It was Prince Kraa who gave voice to the thing that lay in the minds of each of us in that moment.

"This . . . *this* . . . is the road to Yhoom."

12. Into the Abyss

There was never any question but that we should descend into the great pit. Let the dwarf Dhu howl of blasphemy as he would, or Kraa murmur of the curse of the gods, or even stout Kuruk, his face a mask of superstitious fear, mumble half-forgotten verses from the ancient epics—*we had to see what was down there.*

The man would not have been fully human who could have turned away from that world-deep pit without striving to learn what world-old mystery lay hidden in its depths.

We took food and water, weapons and sleeping gear, leaving all else behind. The Bronston lamps we distributed between us, hanging them on the belts of our thermal suits by hooks designed for just such a purpose.

The stone stair was not easy to get to, lying all the way across the huge chamber; but a ledge of naked rock ran along the inner wall of the holy of holies. With great care we inched our way around the room to the platform, over the edge of the abyss, where the steps started down.

The steps of the stair were broad and shallow, and the stair itself was solid rock. In the dry, cold air no mold or moss or lichen grew here to make our footing slippery or unsafe. Only a man afflicted with vertigo would have felt any fear at entrusting himself to the stair.

For added safety, though, we kept close to the inner wall of the shaft and used the guard lines to tie ourselves together, just as mountaineers rope themselves together into a living chain, so that if one climber should slip and fall, the others could catch the line and save him.

For no particular reason, it was Bolgov who went first. He was the strongest of us all, I suppose, and he went warily, shining his lamp before him to study his footing.

And so we started down; outside, the day was nearly ended. Soon night would fall, black winged, over the ancient world whose thousand mysteries we had only begun to penetrate. But in all the numberless ages since the first night had fallen on the bright dawn of creation, I doubt if any man had ever embarked on a more weird and wondrous journey.

Our legs soon learned the rhythm and spacing of the stair. We lost all fear of falling or stumbling. At first we went down from step to step with exaggerated caution, sliding our shoulders against the smooth rock wall. But with time, repetition alleviated those fears, and we continued our descent more nimbly and with less hesitation. In truth, there was nothing to fear. The stair itself was cut from the solid bedrock of the planet, and the steps were broad enough for us to have made the descent three abreast.

Yhoom . . .

Always I had considered it a myth, nothing more. The Underworld of the Gods, the region of the dead? Well, every race had some such netherworld in its legends. There was the Egyptian underworld of Amenti, to which Anubis conducted the spirits of the dead, and where their hearts were tested in the balance against the Feather of Truth, under the stern eyes of Osiris and of Thoth . . . and the shadowy ghostlands of Sheol, in the myths of the primitive Hebrews . . . the grim Avernus of the Romans . . . and dark Hades of the Greeks . . . even the subterranean realms of Hel in the old Scandinavian sagas.

And the Doctor's remark, noting the similarity between Ilionis and Babylon, made me think of the many nations that had dwelt in Mesopotamia, each sharing an identical myth of the Underworld. I remembered the subterranean region of the dead to which Ishtar descended, to win back the spirit of her perished lover, Tammuz, just as the Greek myths told how Orpheus once went down to the gloom of

Hades to beg the release of his bride, Eurydice, from Pluto and Persephone.

I remembered too the even older Sumerian epic which told of the goddess Inanna who went weeping down into the netherworld of *Na-an-gub*, the "Great Below," to implore the remorseless King of Shadows to return her beloved to the upper world again. And there came into my mind the lines of an old translation of the Sumerian epic I had read many years ago:

> From the great above to the great below,
> the goddess, from the great above to the great below,
> Ishtar, from the great above to the great below,
> descendeth.

As we went down into the darkness, the verses of the old Sumerian poem echoed over and over in my mind.

> From the land of light to the land of darkness,
> to the Netherworld she descended . . .

Step by step, we went down into a gloomy vastness no less strange and awesome than that into which the goddess had gone in the ancient poem. And I remembered to what she had come at last, her journey ended.

> My lady abandoned heaven, abandoned earth,
> to the Netherworld she came,
> to the dark house of Nergal,
> to the seven-gated palace.

> Before the shadow-throne she knelt,
> to him who sat thereon she spake:
> "O Nergal, lord of darkness,
> prince of shadows, hear my mission.
> To the Netherworld have I come . . ."

My mind brooding on one of the oldest of all stories, I strode on down into the blackness, step after step after step.

From time to time we halted to rest and eat a little and moisten our throats with water. On Earth such an ordeal would have been exhausting. Here on Mars, in this cold, dry air, weighing but a fraction of our normal weight, we were fatigued enough, but it was not the grueling ordeal it might have been.

On one such rest stop Dr. Keresny called another mystery to our attention.

"Have you noticed the walls of the shaft?" he inquired. "However this pit came to be, it was no natural cataclysm, no cavern hollowed out by geological forces."

He was right, of course. The shaft was four sided, the walls themselves smooth and regular. Far *too* smooth and regular to have been the work of nature. For that matter, too smooth and regular to have been the handiwork of man! At least, not the work of man armed with any tools known to me: I pointed this out to him, in return.

"You're right, my boy . . . marvelous! The rock is as smooth as glass. Not so much as the scratch of a single chisel stroke to mar its perfect regularity . . . amazing!"

It was amazing. It was also a little frightening. For I could not believe that either natural forces or the work of men could have hollowed out this world-deep shaft that went down and down to the very bottom of the world.

And that left only . . . the supernatural.

Had this abyss been the work of the gods themselves, the Timeless Ones?

But that was nonsense, of course. There are no gods.

Or *are* there?

I had thought Ilionis a myth, but we had walked its shadow-thronged way and looked upon the sepulchers of its long-forgotten kings . . .

I had believed dim Yhoom nothing but a legend, but even now we were descending into its gloomy vastnesses . . .

If two myths are proven true, dare you question the reality behind a third?

Into the Netherworld we descended . . .

When we were simply too weary to continue any further

that night, we slept, huddled against the wall of the pit, wrapped in our sleeping furs, taking guard by turns.

And woke hours later to continue on down.

There was no such thing as day or night here, no sun to lighten our path, no moons to glimmer through the night. And as we continued on down, the air grew richer in oxygen and warmer.

"Ivo, I believe we can dispense with these accursed masks," Keresny said to me. I let them remove their respirators, and they seemed to take no hurt from it. I suppose the air would, in fact, grow thicker and more breathable at the depth we had now reached; and if any heat lurks at the heart of Mars, it would be warmer down here, which it was. So we went on in relative comfort now. Indeed, before long we began to feel almost uncomfortable, so much warmer had the abyss become. We unseamed our thermal suits at the throat, and the Martians threw off their heavy cloaks.

We had no instruments to measure the rate of our descent, nor could we accurately estimate the depth to which we had come by this time. But surely we had penetrated more deeply beneath the surface of the planet than had any man before us.

An amusing thought struck me, and I grinned. I was not going to enjoy climbing all the way back up to the temple again! Maybe we could find a shortcut . . .

We went on down, losing track of the hours after a time, losing all notion of day and night.

I noticed that my watch had stopped. That was odd, because the bead-sized energy cell was supposed to power it forever. Not that it really mattered very much, I suppose, but the thought did trouble me faintly. It was a sort of omen, somehow. As if we had crossed beyond the barriers of time.

As if we now stood in eternity . . .

And then, all at once, we came to a place where there were not any more stairs leading down.

It took us a few moments to comprehend the fact, for by this point we were so accustomed to following that vast, endless, zigzagging stairway down and down that it was hard to realize the truth.

We had come to the bottom.

And we stood at the threshold of an amazing world.

First we were conscious of a sense of indescribable *depth,* as if we had descended into the very core of the planet and somehow sensed the ponderous weight of all those millions of tons of stone and metal that hung above us. This depth sensation was quite beyond anything in my experience; a queer oppressiveness hovered in the air. I felt like weary Atlas, shouldering up the heavens.

Then we became gradually aware that there was light, even at this depth. A dim saffron glow, sourceless, and casting no shadow. As our eyes slowly became accustomed to the queer yellowish radiance, we found it shone from outcroppings of some flaky, quartzlike mineral that bulged from the walls of the cavern here and there. These bosses of unknown crystal or metal were perhaps radioactive or at least phosphorescent. We could put no name to the glimmering stuff, which did nothing to detract from the oppressiveness we all felt.

As we became used to the queer saffron glow, we began to see just where we were. We stood at the foot of the stone stair, at one end of an immense cavern whose stony roof arched far above our heads. Directly above us yawned the black pit: ahead of us lay the trackless unknown.

"Here too, notice?" Keresny breathed. "None of this is natural; it is all the work of intelligence, but God help us, what science could have wrought on this scale?"

He was right: the floor of the cavern had the same glossy and unnatural smoothness we had noted in the walls of the shaft. Never had I dreamed the science of the Ancients had attained the mastery of such forces as could have hollowed out this enormity at the world's core!

We went forward toward the center of the vast cavern. Our boots rang on the glassy paving; echoes boomed and gibbered up the titanic dome and died in shuddering whispers overhead.

And then another marvel!

Suddenly radiance flared up about us. Far above our heads, globes of dark metal flashed with brilliance. Light blossomed from huge spheres that hung or hovered high at the narrow peak of the dome.

It was darkly crimson, that light, like the blood shed from ruptured and dying suns. But in the brilliant, sanguinary glare the dimmer saffron radiance of the mineral bosses waned and died. The spheres of ruby light were seven in number, and as they bloomed into fire, fat Huw blanched.

"*Aiii,* brothers!" the little minstrel whimpered. "Now are we come unto the very Underworld of the Timeless Ones! Know you not the old tales? Those are the Seven Scarlet Suns that lighten the impenetrable darkness of Yhoom!"

We gaped, craning our necks to observe the remarkable phenomenon. The seven spheres of ruby brilliance were set in a vast ring, a gyre of captive, crimson suns, and by their very light we could see clearly that they hovered without visible support high in the air. None could say what miracle of science or sorcery supported them aloft.

Kuruk clutched my arm in a viselike grip.

"Lord—look!" he breathed.

As if only the bloody radiance shed by the hovering ring of glowing orbs could render it visible, a pathway melted slowly into view. A zone of lambent scarlet luminosity ran as straight as a paved road from the foot of the stone stair where we stood across the immensity of the domed cavern to its farthest side, where a black, hemispherical opening yawned in the cavern wall. One moment before no pathway had been visible: now it blazed ominously before us.

"I gather that we are expected to travel in that direction," the Doctor surmised wryly.

We examined the red way curiously. So far as we could tell by sight and touch alone, it was the same dark, adamantine, glassy smooth substance that paved the entire floor of the vast and echoing cavern. Perhaps the zone of lambent red had been painted there with some chemical which fluoresces to visibility only under the sanguine glare of the ringed artificial suns.

"Well, what're we waitin' for?" Bolgov grunted. "Nothin' around here, so let's follow it and see where it leads."

We switched off our Bronston lamps, as the bloody light from above seemed to provide sufficient illumination. We removed the length of line that had roped us together against the danger of falling and packed these things away in our gear, which we left behind us at the foot of the stairs.

I hesitated, then took up the Iron Crown wrapped in its sacred cloth. This I decided to bear with me, not only because I did not like to be parted from the precious thing, but because some intuition told me I might yet have occasion to use my Power before this weird adventure came to its conclusion.

Prince Kraa and the others retained their weapons, although Dhu argued that to go armed into the presence of the Timeless Ones was sacrilege. The Moon Dragon Prince dismissed this curtly.

"When a man ventures into the unknown, he is a fool to go unarmed," he said. "But if the priest Dhu fears the sin of sacrilege, he may remain behind to guard our packs."

The priest stiffly said he would accompany us, if only to intercede with the gods to spare us from their wrath. Kraa grinned and said nothing.

And so we set forth upon the scarlet way, under the glare of the imprisoned suns, to explore the mysteries of Yhoom.

13. Yhoom

The strange, bloody light made it difficult to make out any details and drowned all colors into tones of gray or brown or black. We crossed the cavern without mishap and approached the odd, hemispherical opening to which the glowing pathway led.

As we neared, we saw that a black, gauzy curtain hung

across this portal. A vague uneasiness bade me caution the others against approaching it too quickly. I went forward alone and examined it carefully, not touching it.

" 'Tis no fabric at all, but a sort of shadow," the boy Chaka marveled. And he was right; a phantom web of darkness stretched across the curious doorway, blocking our access and obscuring whatever lay beyond the portal from our scrutiny.

Huw roused himself, blinking sleepily.

"Eh, brothers! Have you not heard of the Web of Woven Shadows that hangs before the Bridge whereover the spirits of the dead must venture to judgment?"

An ominous cold radiated from the dark barrier. Whatever the thing was, I felt apprehensive and did not think it wise to try passing through it. Keresny stepped to where I stood and peered at the insubstantial screen of darkness.

"It could be a force barrier of some kind," he speculated. "It cancels the vibrations of light or is somehow opaque to them—if only I had a subelectronic scanner with me, I could ascertain the nature of the screen!"

I donned the Crown and drew my Power about me like a mantle, while the others stepped back. The thought crystals set in the head piece vastly augment the mental powers of the wearer, and I thrust out at the web of darkness with the magnified power of my mind, sensing the interplay of strange forces—

And without warning the barrier of darkness was gone!

Had my telepathic probe triggered some response within the mechanism, or was the Web timed to cease operation at the approach of sentient beings? To these questions we had no answers. We went on, striding through the vast arch of dark stone without harm.

We emerged into another cavernous space, but here darkness reigned and no gyre of captive scarlet suns strove against the gloom. Moreover, the ground was rough and broken, and we began to wish we had brought the Bronston lamps with us, although none of us desired to retrace our steps to get them.

A dim greenish light strengthened about us, as our eyes adjusted to the dark. But this radiance shone from no ring of luminous spheres, but from a weird forest of hulking and monstrous growths.

As the clumped and towering shapes became clearly visible, we halted in amazement. For this queer forest was not of trees, but of fungoid growths—tremendous mushrooms, thousands of times greater than anything we had seen. The fungi that grow on the surface of Mars are stunted, hardy forms: here in the warm, humid, richer air, they attained truly monstrous proportions.

Most of the stalked monstrosities that loomed up in our way were hooded in ominous scarlets, their smooth, glistening flesh mottled with poisonous hues. The weird fungoid growths swayed slightly to our step, and their repellent shapes and the semenlike odor that exhuded from them, as from morels, brought to mind swaying and hooded vipers and the musky stench of cobras.

Mastering our almost instinctive revulsion, we stepped gingerly into the fungus forest. The ground was a crawling mass of fleshy tubers and sprouting fungi that squelched wetly underfoot, releasing a slimy, nauseous odor. But we went on, finding a pathway that wound between the obscene, glistening trunks. Overhead, like ghastly flowers of abnormal size, such as might flourish in a wizard's garden, the hoods of ominous crimson, sharp yellow, or virulent green swayed and rustled.

The dim and sickly light that shone dully from the monstrous growths may have been a natural luminosity or the phosphorescence of decay; we could not be certain. But by its ghastly light our features assumed a livid hue, like the faces of long-dead cadavers. And again Huw hearkened back to the legends of his people: "Aiii, brothers! Is it not all as the ancient legends tell? First, the Black Pit and at its bottom, the Zone of Saffron Light; and then the Cavern of the Seven Scarlet Suns, and beyond that, the green-litten abyss of Yhuu. Just as the sagas described it all!"

The Martians muttered amongst themselves. The old Prince was worried, and Kuruk looked grim enough, but terror shone nakedly in the glistening eyes and quivering features of the little hunchbacked priest.

Only the boy Chaka gazed around him eagerly, bright

eyes filled with wonder and delight at the strangeness through which we passed.

Ilsa stumbled, her feet slipping in the slimy tangle of the wormlike growths that squirmed underfoot. In staggering to recover her balance, she stumbled against a squat puff-ball, whose heavy head nodded and burst into a clinging cloud of musty-smelling spores. We slapped them from her clothing, but they flew into our faces and made us cough and sneeze.

But she took no harm from the cloud of spores; and we went on into a subterranean world whose mystery deepened about us with every step.

In time the repulsive forest of giant mushrooms thinned out, and we came to its borders. We were happy to be free of the stench and slime of the monster fungi, but as we continued ahead, we began to regret the sickly green phosphorescence, whose dim luminosity extended no farther than the borders of the weird forest itself.

We went forward gingerly into unbroken darkness.

The floor of this cavern was broken and cluttered, and round, hollow things crunched underfoot. I am glad we had no light by which to see just what they were, for I have the feeling that they were *skulls*—but whether human or those of some beast native to this hellish region, I could not even guess.

"Eh now, and if the sagas continue to foretell what lies in our path as truthfully as they have until now," Huw wheezed at my shoulder, "this Zone of Darkness should end ere long, and we will emerge to find ourselves before the Bridge of Fire . . ."

After a long time a dim, pulsing redness gleamed ahead of us. It was a dull ghost of light—as if some titan had crushed a giant ruby under its thumb and smeared the smouldering gem dust across the blackness.

We emerged at length into a colossal space whose height or extremities we could not see. Deep, crimson fires pulsed slowly, waxing and waning, like the throbbing of a tremendous heart. And we saw before us yet another vision drawn from the world-old myths of Mars.

The stony floor of this immensity was cleft asunder by a broad chasm of unplumbed gloom. Up from this pit a cold dank wind blew without ceasing. And spanning the chasm from rim to rim arched a fantastic thing of throbbing jeweled fire.

"The Bridge of Fire!"

It was beautiful and terrible beyond description—beyond belief! All of jeweled minerals was it made, glittering with crystals whose thousand facets blazed with rhythmic fires. Of every shade of rubescence were these crystalline minerals . . . from the faintest ghost pink of early dawn, through the salmon-pink that glows within certain seashells . . . through red-orange and flaming scarlet . . . dark and sullen crimsons, like congealing blood . . . to the deepening purples that lay at the edge of the spectrum of visible light.

All of many million gems was this arch of fiery brilliance fashioned, ranging in size from gems as small as sand grains up to crystals of monstrous and abnormal girth, larger than human arms could encompass.

And the same gemlike fires that flickered in each single stone pulsed to the same throbbing rhythm!

Keresny's face was blank with awe.

"Could such a miracle of nature be merely the work of geological forces?" he whispered. "And yet surely it must —for how could such a thing be the work of man?"

We stared in silence, drinking in the wonder of the bridge of beauty . . . And my mind wandered back to the old myths of Earth, to the Bifrost Bridge that spans the dizzy gap between the worlds of Men and of the godlike Aesir, the rainbow bridge of Norse epic and myth . . . and I thought of shining Serat, the sword-slender bridge of gleaming metal Allah flung across the gulf of Hell, and whereover the spirits of the dead must pass to attain to the blissful gardens of Mohammed's paradise . . .

We tested the blazing thing for strength, and it was solid beneath our feet. So we ventured forth upon the glittering arch. Underfoot, we trod gemmy fires that might have adorned the splendid crowns of czars and sultans. We went on, inching our way across the brilliant curve of pulsing light, and every hue in the red segment of the spectrum flashed beneath our feet, from the hard scarlet of Chinese lacquer to the royal crimson that burns in the cloaks of emperors to the rich, deep, Tyrian purple that only the immortal caesars of Rome might wear.

Beneath us, the glittering mass of jewels blossomed with incredible splendors of every ruby shade . . . rose and coral, the elusive orange flame that glimmers within the opal . . . ruby and garnet and the delicate pink blush that stains the rare fire pearl. It was a dream of gorgeous fable we trod, that soaring arch of brilliant fire that spanned the gloom-drowned abyss . . . and at its end we found an even greater wonder.

The throbbing ruby glow shone from behind us now; we moved out into a great cavern whose floor was cluttered with curious shapes. But for these we had as yet no eyes— they were drawn to that which rose before us!

A circular pit was cut in the stony floor; within it, from wall to wall, amber mists coiled, but they were—*frozen.* A dim wall of translucent, clouded golden crystal and set deep within, three weird figures hung suspended, like flies trapped in oozy amber.

The Three were inhumanly tall and gaunt, their attenuated limbs motionless. Naked were they of the slightest adornment, but their elongated bodies were sexless. Like —and yet unlike—both Earthman and Martian were the Three and alien to either. For minute, sparkling scales dusted their slender limbs and torsos, like flakes of glinting, lucent mica.

The more we looked, the further divergences we saw from the human norm. The Three possessed hands, but they were nine fingered and had two more joints than our own and utterly lacked nails. Their smooth, narrow chests were devoid of nipples, and their flat bellies had no navels . . . They were not mammals, as are both Martian and Earthmen, but *reptilian,* for all the anthropoid design of their bodies.

They hung there, frozen in the amber crystal, and we could see that the heads and faces of the Three were the least humanlike portion of their strange anatomies. Narrow and long and elfin were those faces, with sharply pointed jaws, high, ridged cheekbones, noses as long and thin as knife blades, lipless and curiously *triangular* mouths—faces dusted all over with minute scales of lucent gold.

The brow ridges of their faces were arched and very prominent, and above these their heads bulged in twin, swelling, hairless globes, cleft into two rounded lobes or bosses by a curious division down the center of the brow.

Beneath those arched brow ridges the eyes of the Three were open and stared into our own with a fathomless gaze.

Green as the depths of perfect emeralds were those eyes and undivided, as are our own, into whites and pupils: and many times more large than human eyes . . . depthless, tapering orbs of lambent jade, wherein your gaze sank endlessly, until you blinked awake and snatched your gaze away from those hypnotic wells of dim green fire with a start.

They seemed to have no ears at all; at least no protuberances or orifices we could see.

One of the Three held in his supple, nine-fingered hand a glittering thing. A hoop of pure crystal, struck across with crystal bars from which hung tiny rings of glassy stuff. A crossbar and a handle, also of crystal, completed the curious instrument. It reminded me of the mystic *crux ansata,* the Looped Cross, which the ancient Egyptians called the *ankh,* the Cross of Life. It reminded me also of the sistrum used by the priests of the Nile in certain ceremonies . . .

We said nothing to each other.

We knew who the three gaunt mummies frozen in the misted amber expanse of crystal were—or who they had been aeons before.

The Timeless Ones . . .

The features of the strange trinity were vacant, and the eyes were dull and lifeless. But their visages, alien though they might be, bore the marks of wisdom and kindness, gentleness and even humor.

It was very easy to see why men should have thought them gods, and worshiped their memories through long ages.

We turned our eyes away, and there was nothing to say.

We looked about us, and then it was that our eyes lighted upon the fabulous treasure of the Ancients we had come so far and endured so much to find.

For this cavern too the old Martians had devised a name.

The Den of Miracles . . .

And marvels and wonders lay about us to every side . . . treasures out of the past of an ancient world . . . miracles that old myths had only whispered of.

Just beyond where Bolgov stood, a vast hoop of shining, chrome-bright metal clasped a clouded disc of milky jade. Beyond, a slender rod of nameless indigo metal gleamed faintly, tipped with a cone of shimmering brass. A sphere of dew-clear crystal lay cupped in prongs of black metal.

Keresny gazed about him with puzzled eyes.

Wonderingly he touched a huge cylinder of gleaming white metal or porcelain or some strange synthetic. From its pointed crest, Medusa tresses of coppery coils fell away.

The things lay all about us, cluttering the cavern floor; large and small they were, of plastic and ceramic, of metal and glass and crystal. Some were of the sleek simplicity of a Brancusi sculpture, others a complexity of design so bewildering the eye could scarcely grasp it all.

They had the look of alien machines . . . instruments of an unknown and extraplanetary science . . .

And that, of course, is what they were.

Amazement and delight grew in the Doctor's features as he began to realize this. I think it dawned on all of us at once, for we looked at one another, and simultaneously we began to laugh until the tears flowed down our cheeks.

We had come on a sordid treasure hunt for gold and gems.

But we had found, instead, something a million times more valuable than any treasure of mere gold could ever be: the lost scientific miracles of the Ancients! The wonder mechanisms of a mysterious people of time's dawn, who had wrought with strange powers the forgotten art whereof the thought records and the Iron Crown were the only artifacts still known. And it lay all about us, heaped and mounded and untouched by time!

The release of tension, the burst of clean, healthy laughter that welled up in us, was touched with hysteria. We laughed and laughed, clapping each other's shoulders. I reached out and gathered Ilsa to me and kissed her soundly, until she was flushed and breathless.

But one of us had no laughter.

We turned, curiously, just as he spoke in cool, heavy tones that cut across our mood of hilarity like a spray of icy water.

"Ivo Tengren, Josip Keresny, you are under arrest in the name of the Mandate."

Kuruk had no knowledge of our tongue, but he sensed the menace. He growled deep in his chest and reached for the hilt of his sword. I laid one hand on his arm, arresting the motion.

Because it was Bolgov. And he had a gun.

And I groaned inwardly, cursing myself: I had forgotten about that laser gun and forgotten my determination to take it from him. The thought had passed through my mind . . . and then I had gone on to other things!

Now I wished most desperately that I had remembered about the gun. But now it was too late!

Keresny understood none of this. He frowned at Bolgov, bewilderedly.

"Konstantin, what are you doing?"

The big man answered crisply, saying he was a Star-class agent of the AN Space Mandate. But I was not really listening to his words: I was watching him, half-bemusedly, thinking to myself how very little we know about those around us. How long was it now, since that afternoon they had first approached my table, there in the arcade at Venice?—only thirty days, only a month? For the past month then, I had spent my days and nights in the company of the black-bearded Ukrainian; eaten by his side, ridden in his company, slept near him. And never once had I seen the real man behind the imposture; he had seemed a surly, grumbling lout, a sort of a caricature.

Looking at him now as he stood cool and steady, eyes alert, amused, wary, hand rock-steady and unwavering on the gun, I knew that he had only been acting a part all those weeks. And never once had I seen through it!

He was talking to the bewildered Keresny; I began to listen again.

". . . wandering commission, with no one to report to, no superior. We got wind of something up, something you had found in Thoth-Nepenthes on your last trip. Mars is in an explosive state right now, and any Earthside visitor is watched carefully, for Tengren's cause has aroused surprising support among the Liberals and the Universalist party."

"I? But—I never said a word of my discovery!" the Doctor protested. Bolgov's black eyes twinkled with amusement.

"You didn't have to! Your very actions were suspicious in themselves. With still ten days to go before your visitor's visa expired, you suddenly closed down excavations, abandoned the site, and came hotfooting it back to Syrtis, leaving the planet almost immediately. Once back in Luna City, you retired from the museum and went to France to live with your granddaughter. The most cursory study of your activities, however, showed that you were nosing about the gray labor market, searching for a reliable space pilot who could handle a Mars skimmer and who had maybe been in a bit of trouble somewhere, so that he was not likely to ask too many questions. It was simplicity itself to set myself in your path and to get myself hired by you.

"I must admit, I hardly expected you to spill the whole story of the treasure to me that first day. But now that we had some idea of what you were on to, I decided to just go along for the ride and let you find the treasure for us, if there was any to be found. Then, when you got the notion to get Tengren to help you, in return for an illicit one-way ticket back to Mars, things got more and more interesting.

We have been anxious to catch Tengren out of bounds ever since his trial; we want him behind bars where he can't get into any mischief. So here we are! I will admit, though, I never expected this thing to lead to anything quite like *this*," he smiled, nodding at the weird machines that loomed about us in the vague light.

"You're just one man with a gun," I pointed out. "Maybe you can herd us at gunpoint back up the stair to the surface again and maybe not. There are eight of us you'll have to keep your eye on, you know."

"Maybe I'll try harder, Cat-lover," he chuckled. My lips tightened.

"Maybe you will. You may get us all to the surface again, but do you really think you can get out of this, even if you manage to get that far? How are you going to get past all of Prince Kraa's warriors, who are encamped outside the temple?"

"Maybe it won't be quite as much of a problem as you seem to think," he said. "Maybe I'll have a little help."

Training the cold black eye of the laser gun on us, rock-steady in one capable hand, he fumbled inside the open throat of his thermal suit and drew out a flat black case of plastic and metal which he showed us, smilingly.

My heart sank, for I knew what it was. A beeper—an ultrawave radio beacon. He recognized from my expression that I knew the thing.

"Two police boats have been following us from the last five days," he said, "ever since we left Farad."

"I thought . . . Ivo said no craft could fly above the plateau," Keresny faltered. "Too dangerous . . . the gas geysers . . ."

"That may be true enough for skimmers," replied Bolgov, "but these are space boats. They can go anywhere, land anywhere, and they pack enough punch to handle almost anything. I doubt if a couple dozen Cat-men, armed with bronze knives, can stand up very long under a barrage of ship-mounted lasers."

He was right, of course. The Moon Dragon warriors were gallant men, and they would fight bravely. They would die, fighting bravely; but they would still die.

So it was defeat then . . . and just as we stood on the very threshold of victory. Well, it had happened before; but this time it was ended for good. They would never let me walk away from this debacle.

The irony of it was that this time I had come within an inch of success! For the mysterious mechanisms that loomed all around us in the dimness represented an arsenal of super-weapons left behind by the Ancients. Not all of them were weapons, most likely, but some of them must have been. And I did not doubt that the sages and savants of the People could puzzle out the secrets of their ancestors—could learn to awaken and direct these mystery weapons from time's dawn—and with them we could shatter the strength of the Mandate on Mars forever, sweep the CA cops from every foot of this world, hurl them back to Earth.

Surely, enough of the ancient wisdom and the ancient science was stored in this one room to free Mars from its oppressors and keep it free forever!

And now this bright dream, like all the others I had dreamed, was dimmed and would die too.

14. When Sleepers Wake

It was just at that moment, as I stood there with the bitter taste of defeat on my tongue, that an eerie music woke and sang.

A faint, weird strain of unearthly melody rang through the cavern . . . the mere ghost of chiming bells, a tuneless crystalline ringing.

And the gun in Bolgov's hand—*exploded.*

There was a deafening retort and a momentary flash of blinding glare.

Bolgov screeched, clutching fingers seared to the bone in a spray of white-hot droplets of incandescent metal.

The stench of cooked flesh was heavy in our nostrils. He fell to his knees, whimpering at the pain.

Giving voice to a deep, booming cry of joyous fury, Kuruk pounced on the huddled figure of the Ukrainian and knocked him sprawling with one blow of big, hammerlike fists.

Again that faint, trilling music as of wind-blown crystal bells, chiming sweetly, came to our ears.

I was looking at Ilsa, at the dawning awe and wonder in her blue eyes. My gaze flashed to Prince Kraa, who had fallen to his knees suddenly and Chaka and hunched Dhu beside him.

Bland, lazy Huw still stood, his face gaping, eyes staring at some wondrous sight behind me, where the great mass of smoky amber crystal rose from the pit in the floor, prisoning within it the three gaunt, alien figures of the dead gods.

I turned and saw—*glory!*

Amber crystal dissolved to whorls of amber mist! Coiling golden vapor, mixed with whirling clouds of tiny, glittering motes of starry fire . . . like the dazzling dust of diamonds or a mist composed of scintillant atoms of golden fire . . .

The crystal was frozen no more!

Still the impossibly slender bodies hovered in their places, but now the hard, frozen, impenetrable crystal that had sheathed them was gone. Now warm, amberous mists swirled about them—a vortex of glittering motes spun and seethed about the figures, which hovered weightlessly amidst insubstantial vapors.

And now they—*lived!*

I did not understand it then nor do I understand it now.

But the golden, diamond-moted mists boiled—writhed —coiled—and parted!

And we could see them plainly now, the tall, the slim, the inhumanly slender, bright-scaled bodies, naked and sexless looking for all the world like those attenuated sculptures Giacometti had wrought a century ago

Whatever the trancelike condition, whatever the stasis or state of suspended animation, that had held them frozen and preserved amidst the smoky, clouded mass of amber crystal, the spell was broken now, and the Timeless Ones were—*awake!*

Their alien faces were alive with expression, vivid with emotions. Faces so very alien and strange to us, but faces filled with warmth and compassion—yes, and with humor too.

Ageless wisdom shone in those enormous, depthless eyes of lambent emerald; stern, kingly justice too, and a sympathy and understanding that seemed almost godlike in their breadth.

Their narrow chests rose and fell as they breathed. The green lamps of their eyes moved over us, reading the naked pain and terror of Bolgov's eyes, where he groveled under Kuruk's heavy hand, nursing his scalded hand to his breast.

And they—*spoke!* Not with voices, not with words, but through the medium of pure thought. Minds vast and cool and ageless reached out to us, projecting a message into our own minds with startling force and clarity.

Who are you nine who stand before us in our secret place and disturb our slumbers with your passions and discords and violence?

O, strange—strange!—to hear an alien thought echo through your own mind!

The tone of the mental message was a clear, sweet, singing as of icy winds gusting through sharp, needlelike pinnacles of frozen crystal on some wintry world. Inhumanly cold and sweet and singing was the voice that spoke in our brains—the voice of the Timeless Ones!

But brilliant eyes of green flame softened—softened—and compassion warmed the cold, wild music of their thoughts.

You are all brothers! Why, then, do you threaten, why do you injure one another? Have our teachings fallen upon deaf ears? Can it be the children of this age have forgotten us, have turned aside from our teachings? Is the law we taught you, when first we came amongst you in olden times, followed no longer by the children of this age?

I opened my mouth to speak, to say something but—

how do you explain a hundred million years of human history to godlike, passionless beings?

How do you describe hatred, cruelty, injustice, greed, bigotry and—*evil*—to bright, immortal, unfallen spirits who have tasted none of the darker passions of men?

But I did not even have to try.

Their eyes moved from one of us to another, noting the differences, seeing that Earthman and Martian stood before their age-old tomb in the Den of Miracles.

There is a strangeness here . . . We have slept long, too long, it may be . . . What has happened to the world while we but withdrew from it to slumber for a time and thus renew ourselves?

Cold fingers touched the periphery of my mind; tendrils of eerie and alien thought insinuated themselves into the pattern of my memories. I saw Ilsa start and touch her brow with wondering fingers as she felt the gentle invasion too.

What things are these have happened while we slept? Conquest, slavery, rebellion, war . . . Do you not know you both be brothers, children of Earth and children of Mars, alike?

Their sharp features grew stern as they fingered through our thoughts, reading of Earth's subjugation of Mars, of her exploitation of her sister world. Warmth died in those great green eyes as they read the story of my ordeal and struggle to free Mars from her oppressors.

We have slept long, it seems . . . Millions of years of time have passed, as you children reckon time . . . It sorrows us that you have warred against each other . . . When all this world was young and rich with life, we came hither from our own world, lost to us and ruined forever . . . And we chose a little animal with wide, wondering eyes and guided him upward on the path toward thought, so that his companionship might assuage our own loneliness . . . and those of our own race, who fled inward, nearer to the sun, to the green world with the great blue seas . . .

Dr. Keresny gasped, his face alive with incredulous amazement.

"*Aster!*" he exclaimed, eagerly. "The lost, fifth planet

that some believe once existed between the orbits of Mars and Jupiter and whose wreckage forms the Asteroid Zone —is that the lost, ruined home world of which you speak? I cannot project my thoughts as you, but perhaps—"

It is not needed; speak aloud and we can sense your meaning . . . Yes, we read the data in your memory lattice . . . The fifth planet was our lost and golden home . . . There were those among us who unwisely sought to tamper with cosmic forces beyond our control, the strange balance and flux of forces that sustain the worlds in their paths about the parent sun . . . These forces escaped from the grasp of those who would manipulate them, and the resultant convulsion tore our golden world asunder and scattered its ruin afar . . . We three survived and two of our brethren, who voyaged sunward to your green Earth . . .

"Then you Three guided human evolution here on Mars," I broke in, "while on Earth, also, the two Timeless Ones guided the rise of intelligence there!"

It is so . . . Our brothers too, we see, chose a warmblooded little animal . . . And since you are brothers, Earthmen and Martians, it troubles us that you would war upon and ravage one another, when peace and brotherhood should live between you . . .

"We of Mars would live in peace with Earth, but she holds us captive," I said.

Then we must undo this thing and sever your chains, for there is from of old, from the very beginning, a friendship between us and the folk of this world . . .

It was then that Bolgov made his play!

He had crouched there, nursing his hurt hand, his face white and taut with desperation, eyes filled with terror as he saw the solemn golden figures move and breathe and live. He too felt the mental message they projected; and he knew that time was running out.

Suddenly he tore himself loose from the grip of Kuruk and sprang away to one side, clawing at the black case under his clothing. He got it out somehow, and a thrill of horror went through me, as I thought of those police boats hovering out there above the Lost City.

Triumph gleamed in his eyes as he fumbled with the beacon. Ilsa stifled a cry, and Kuruk lunged for the case.

But Bolgov winced, features contorting with pain. His seared fingers could not hold the ultrawave projector, and it fell—and Kuruk was upon him again, bludgeoning him senseless with one smashing blow of those heavy fists. We breathed easily, tension draining from us.

Then we saw who it was had snatched the fallen signal from Bolgov's hand.

Dhu!

Malignant fires gleamed in the beady eyes of the hunched little priest. I think he was stark mad then, the reality behind his myths had perhaps proved too much for his sanity to bear. It is often so, with zealots, with fanatics: they walk a narrow bridge, teetering on the brink of madness, and it takes little to dislodge them from their precarious balance.

His hatred of me had burned deep, and it had festered badly. I think it was the fact that I was one of the *F'yagha,* the Hated Ones, that made him hate me so. The thought that an accursed Outworlder could still be the true Jamad Tengru was a sacrilege he could not resolve; it had driven a wedge into his mind, splitting it deeper and deeper asunder.

And now, perhaps, the discovery that Earthman and Martian were not really two separate races at all but were brothers, both children of the Timeless Ones, had driven him beyond the edge of reason into the red howling hell of madness.

For there is no other way to explain the thing he did then.

Glaring with icy, gloating triumph directly into my eyes, the little priest *activated the signal.*

The faint, sweet chiming of crystalline music rang wildly through the cavern—but too late.

The crystal *crux ansata,* the sistrum that had disrupted Bolgov's laser gun, sang again—and the ultrawave beacon shattered in Dhu's hand, littering the stony pave with shards of smoking plastic.

But too late!

There could be no doubt about it—we had all seen Dhu press the signal button in the side of the beeper.

It was Ilsa who turned to the Timeless Ones for aid.

"Oh, please, help us! That alarm summons our enemies, who are armed with frightful weapons of destruction. They will massacre our friends on the surface, who are encamped before the temple and who are armed only with swords."

The Three smiled down at the girl gently.

Comfort yourself, child, and dry your tears! Those who would wreak violence upon others shall perish by it . . . We, who love peace, are yet just . . . And betimes, justice must be harsh and swift . . . Behold!

The long hand that held the crystal sistrum in supple, golden fingers lifted, pointing the *crux ansata* toward one of the huge mechanisms that thronged the Den of Miracles. The mechanism was that huge lens of milky crystal jade, clasped in a great chromelike metal hoop.

The sistrum chimed—once!

This time we were watching as the breath of eerie music was sounded. So this time we saw the swift rings of pallid light that spread, flashing, from the sistrum, like ripples in the surface of a brook. It was like the wild, sweet, tuneless music of the shaken sistrum made visible.

Light awoke in the lens of cloudy jade! The milky substance blurred—cleared—and became a brilliant mirror. Glassed within that lens we saw, somehow reflected from afar by some miracle of alien science we could not even begin to understand, a vision of the surface. It was a perfect image, exact in every detail: night had fallen on the surface of Mars far above this deep cavern where we stood. Stars burned sharp and wintry in the black dome of heaven.

We saw, by their dim luminance, the age-worn ruins of holy Ilionis—the half-collapsed temple—the Moon Dragon warriors camped on its outer stair—and from above we saw descending two sleek ovids of glistening metal, riding down on their landing jets. Inverted fountains of intolerable fire lit the night like twin lightnings—the warriors sprang up in terror, clutching sword and spear and dart tube, futile frail things to set against the ravening fury of laser batteries.

Behold now, children, the justice of the Timeless Ones!

Again the sistrum was shaken!

Again a weird strain of crystalline music, the chiming of pure, faint bells, rang about us!

Again the racing ripples of ever-widening light blazed up from the *crux ansata*—fell, one by one, into the jade mirror—faded there and were gone!

And we looked into the magic mirror; and we looked upon a marvel!

Once, long ago, I saw a film in which an engine had come apart, piece by piece. It was some technical trickery, some feat of clever animation, I know. But that same marvel I saw again in the mirror of the Timeless Ones.

The two police boats came apart in midair.

They came apart all at once.

The fabric disintegrated into a cloud of flying sections. Solid metal suddenly began a spreading cloud of fragments, and those fragments became whorls of glittering metallic dust, and that dust became mere vapor, which spread and spread—dispersed—and was gone!

Fire fountains winked out. Blackness closed down upon the scene. Our eyes adjusted to the lack of those twin brilliances, and we saw the astounded warriors, gesticulating at the empty sky, waving their arms, yelling.

Two police boats had vanished into thin air in a twinkling. Two fast, heavily-armored cruisers, armed with sufficient nuclear might to lay in glowing puddles of half-vaporized metal every city on this planet, had melted away, before nothing more frightful than a single burst of chiming, crystalline music from a shaken sistrum!

A vast relief welled up in me, and something else, something I had almost forgotten existed, something called—*hope.*

Night had fallen, up there on the surface of Mars. But it was a night of gods, when old, long-slumbering powers had waked at last and moved to judgment. Before dawn lit the sky again, much would be changed. An age would end, and a new age would begin, and when dawn blazed forth again, it would shine over a new world.

15. Night of Gods

The disintegration of the two police boats affected each of us in different ways.

Bolgov huddled groggily, face blank, eyes dulled, despair written in his features.

Dhu squatted moaning, froglike face hidden behind shaking hands. He keened softly, and the Timeless Ones regarded him with compassion and tenderness.

That one has a madness . . . Too much hatred can eat at the foundations of sanity like a canker . . . He will rest here a time and sleep . . . And when he wakes again, his mind will be whole.

Keresny was fascinated by this glimpse at an alien technology.

"The vibratory wave set up by the sistrum," he said excitedly, "must somehow cancel the nuclear binding force that holds matter together in a rigid structure. Those two spacecraft literally *vaporized,* but without heat, explosion, or radioactive contamination. What an astounding display of force! How do you suppose they channel and focus the direction of the wave?"

The serene thought projections of the Three sounded again in the depths of our minds.

Now we shall set our decision into action. We are determined that no longer may we permit the children of Earth to subjugate and enslave the children of Mars! All sentient life is one: every intelligent race is the brother of every other . . . We, too, are your brothers, though Elder Brothers, it may be . . . Before this night has ended, the rule of

the Outworlders shall close, and all Earthmen shall depart
from this world forever, and never will they be permitted
to return . . .

I blinked back stinging tears, for this victory was more
complete than that of which I had dreamed, and now it
would be bloodless, as well. We watched as the Timeless
Ones activated another of the mystery machines that stood
gleaming amid the shadows. It was a tall, tapering cylinder
of clear crystal, like an immense glassy tube, taller than a
man. The cold, faint song of the shaken sistrum pealed
once more, and lambent rings of blue light began floating
up through the length of the crystal tube, vanishing at its
top.

The image machine blurred—the scene shifted—and
we looked down at the streets of the nearest of the Colonies, Laestrygonum, as if from some lofty vantage point
high in the heavens above the dim hemispherical haze of
the MPB field.

Night lay deep and dark upon the Colony; the streets
were thick with shadow. But through those streets a
blank-faced horde trudged mechanically. Our viewpoint
swooped down upon a sea of white faces, as empty of voli-
tion as a herd of mindless zombies. From uniform insignia
we recognized that the shuffling mob was made up of
Colonial Administration police, clerks, administrative
workers, and bureaucrats.

They drifted through the dark streets from every direction, and their goal was the terminus of the tractor trains
which led to the debarkation camp. Again the scene shifted with magical suddenness, and we saw the squat profile
of the satellite shuttle on the landing flat, filling up as long
files of Earthmen poured into the hold. As one shuttle
filled to capacity, it lifted off on flaring jets and drifted up
to Deimos, where spacecraft were moored for the crossover to Luna and Earth.

Already the Earthmen were leaving Mars! It was an as-
tonishing sight.

The jade disc of the image machine blurred and then
cleared, showing in swift succession similar scenes taking

place at Syrtis, Sun Lake City, Charontis, Christoffsen Port, Propontis, and the rest of the Twelve Colonies.

Blank-faced, dead-eyed Earthmen—in the thousands! —were flowing back into space, leaving Mars behind, returning to the distant world that had sent them here to loot and plunder, to exploit and to enslave! It was a fantastic sight, and my heart thrilled to see it.

But it was the boy Chaka, of us all, who realized the full implications of the exodus. His bright young mind had extrapolated beyond the obvious, while the rest of us clustered about the huge glimmering lens of the image machine, enthralled by the succession of amazing pictures it revealed to us.

"Lords—Great Ones!" he shrilled. "What of the Jamad? If it is your decree that all of the accursed *F'yagha* are to go home and leave the People to rule their own world—must he too leave us?"

The implications of his words stunned me; frankly it had not even occurred to me that the stern fiat of the Timeless Ones would extend to me as well. Suddenly I saw that it could—that it must!

The Three were sorrowful but adamant.

All of the children of Earth must quit this world, if any go at all . . . For to make an exception in a law is to destroy both its validity and its justice. First, the Jamad must pass the Crown into the hands of another and pronounce the Ritual that is the transferal of sovereignity . . . Then he too must hither to his home . . .

My friends stared at me, flustered and at a loss for words. Kraa was troubled, Huw bewildered. But Kuruk was grimly defiant, and as for the boy, he was on the brink of tears.

Suddenly something welled up within me. I strode forward and raised my arms to the Three where they floated amidst the diamond-moted mists of coiling amber.

"Hear me, Timeless Ones!" I cried. "You are making a mistake—you, who speak of brotherhood are blinded with a kind of bigotry! Let me speak!"

Speak then; we will listen and—judge!..

I strove for calmness, strove to order my thoughts.

"If all sentient races are brothers, despite the superficial differences of tongue or color or creed, then I ask you—is not the planet of their birth also only a superficial difference? Is not a man still a man, whether he be Mars born or Earth born?"

What is it that you are trying to say?

"That there is, by reason and logic and true justice, nothing that sets a man apart from another. There is truly *no* difference between two men, so far as justice can discern. What is it, then, upon which you can fairly and honestly decide this man belongs to Earth and this man to Mars?"

Speak—if you have the answer . . .

Urgency lent my tongue an unaccustomed eloquence.

"I say the only difference between an Earthman and a Martian lies within his heart. For it is therein that he himself selects his own allegiance! An Earthman is one who has chosen the Earth above all worlds; and, conversely, a Martian is one who foreswears all other worlds but Mars!"

They nodded thoughtfully, wise, deep eyes bent upon me. I rushed on, the words tumbling out in desperation.

"Hear me and judge! It is not just for myself that I plead. What of the Colonists themselves? I do not speak of the enslavers, the plunderers, the exploiters, the police, or the government—but the *people* of the Colonies. The simple men, the little men, who have left Earth behind forever, to make Mars their home. Here they have built their homes; here their children have been born; and here—on Mars—they desire to live and die and be buried. By the test that I have just described, are they not as truly men of Mars as are those who stand before you—Kraa, Huw, Kuruk, and Chaka? And what of myself—am I not truly a Martian, in all ways that *really* matter? Have I not foresworn my own people and their ways to join my heart to the People? It is only an accident of birth that makes me native to another world—but I am more truly Martian than many who were lucky enough to have been born one —for I *chose* Mars."

I folded my arms.

"Now—judge me!" I said into the silence.

The way back proved much easier and swifter than the descent had been, for the Timeless Ones whisked us to the surface in a twinkling through another of their many magics.

The Moon Dragon warriors were delighted and relieved to see us again, whole and safe. They were filled with marvels to relate, and among them the miraculous disintegration of the two *F'yagha* spacecraft was the least remarkable. Faces agleam with excitement, they told how all the long night through, the darkness had been cloven with the fiery trails of the *F'yagha* ships, drifting up one by one into the skies atop tails of scintillant flame and thunder.

" 'Tis as if all of the Hated Ones in the world are—are going home!" the chieftain we had left in charge of the warriors swore. We told him that was exactly what was happening.

Dawn broke in the east—the swift, sudden blossoming of light that is morning on Mars. The long Night of Gods was over; a new day had dawned at last.

As for the Timeless Ones, they had returned to their dreams again—but only for a little, they told us. Soon—in a few years or a decade or a century or two—they would awake again and speak to the Princes of the People. Then would they unseal the Den of Miracles and instruct the savants in the use of those instruments and devices whereof a free planet might have need.

We were not really sorry to see the Three return again to the slumbers from which we had roused them in untimely fashion. It is hard enough to begin the task of rebuilding a world—without having the gods peering over your shoulder every moment!

At the gates of Lost Ilionis we made our last farewells. A party of warriors would ride with Dr. Keresny all the long way back to where the *d'Eauville* lay hidden in the Thermodon.

As for Konstantin Bolgov, he would trouble us no more; other guards would ride north to deliver him to Laestrygonum, and from there he could ship out for Earth again. Keresny would find the flight home lengthy and boring, but the computer would do the navigating and piloting for him, and at least, this time, he would not have to worry about being intercepted by a Mandate patrol.

For the patrols were going home too!

The Timeless Ones had decreed that a vast area about Mars was to be closed to all Earth shipping of any kind; only the Jamad himself could terminate this decree, when the time came and he felt that Mars had nothing more to fear from her former oppressors.

If the Doctor was depressed that he had not been permitted by the Timeless Ones to bear any of the treasure of Ilionis back to Earth, he was tactful enough—or realistic enough—to pretend otherwise.

But I think he had found enough to content him. His eyes sparkled with enthusiasm, and he was bubbling over with excitement as we made our last farewells.

"Ah, Ivo, my boy, what a book I shall write when I get back home! Think of it, a lost chapter of human history, rediscovered again . . . The implications to myth, to cosmology, to archaeology, to extraterrestrial historical studies, are immense and fabulous! There will be expeditions launched into the Asteroid Zone because of me. God knows what they will find there . . . Artifacts? records? Perhaps even the ruins of the lost civilization of the Timeless Ones!"

He rubbed his hands together briskly at the thought.

"Oh, Grandfather, I hope there'll be no trouble with the political police," Ilsa said wistfully. "You have broken laws, you know, getting Ivo here. Do you think there will be, well—reprisals?"

He shook his head in a firm negative.

"Nonsense, my dear! Not a chance of it! Why, if anything, they'll be indebted to me back home on Earth. They must be mighty upset, and thoroughly mystified, as the Martian occupational forces come flying back *in toto*, unable to explain what came over them. And they will be somewhat *more* than just mystified when they send patrols back to find out what happened—and run into that 'zone

of no passage' the Timeless Ones have created to go up around Mars, once the last Earth ship has left the vicinity! No, my dear, there'll be no trouble, I'm quite certain of it. Oh, perhaps I did bend a few regulations a little, but I committed no serious crime. And I will be in an excellent position to demand that all charges against me be dropped. For, after all, I will be the only person on Earth who was down there when it all happened, and the only one who knows the full story of the Timeless Ones and their decree as to the freedom of Mars."

His eyes sparkled with excitement.

"Ah, what a book there is to be written! I'll tell the whole story of our expedition in Ilionis and our descent into Yhoom. And after that one there will be other books to write—so many books and so much work to be done! Why, we will have to rewrite the whole history of Mars, as we have it now! And we will perhaps be able to reconstruct the forgotten chronicles of the Ancients by interpreting the old myths and sagas, now that we know they have a genuine basis in truth! Ah . . . there is so much to do; I am anxious to get started with it!"

He beamed on her fondly and a little sadly.

"You are quite certain, my dear, that you will not change your mind? And that you have made the right decision? Keep in mind, my dear, that you will never be able to go back once the zone has gone up . . ."

Ilsa smiled and nodded.

"*Quite* certain, Grandfather!"

Her cheeks were flushed; her eyes sparkled. Yellow locks fluttered around her face like an aureole. Her fingers were warm in mine as we stood hand in hand.

"I will stay here with Ivo," she said. "I too choose Mars!"

He must have seen the tenderness in my face, for he smiled and said slyly: "Perhaps, my dear, Mars has chosen—you! But no matter, no matter. I quite understand—or at least, I think I do. You will have your work cut out for you, both of you, in the years ahead. You need each other now, but you will need each other even more in the hard, long years to come."

I nodded, shaking his hand again.

"Yes, it will be a difficult thing, welding the Nine Nations together into one, healing old breaches, old enmities, and making strangers into friends. But it is a job worth doing, and we shall do the best we can. Perhaps our son, or our son's son, will live in a world united and free and at peace with itself. *That* is a dream worth striving for, don't you think?"

"I do indeed; God speed you in the achieving of it! But now I must go. Ilsa . . . Ivo . . . there are no words, no words at all. Except the old ones: bless you, my children . . . Till we meet again."

He got into the saddle, waved once, and was gone with the warriors of the Moon Dragon riding at his side.

Prince Kraa stared after him, politely baffled.

"*Aii*, I do not understand that man, the *Dok-i-tar!*" he complained.

"What don't you understand, my friend?"

"Him! I thought he came for treasure—he *says* he came for wisdom! And now he departs with nothing at all—and even leaves a woman behind!" The old Prince shook his head in bafflement.

"Never will I understand the ways of the *F'yagha* . . . But now, at last, we are done with them and their strange customs forever—thanks be to the Timeless Ones!"

And so we rode back down the great Avenue of Monoliths to the edge of the Sacred Land, and in time we came again to the gates of Farad.

Had it really been only seven days since we rode out of Farad, bound for the Lost City and the age-old mystery of the Timeless Ones? So much had happened in that little span of time that it was difficult to realize just how short a time it had been.

For in those seven days the future of two worlds had changed forever. An ancient mystery had been solved that had baffled men for ages. A mighty war had been won, and its victory accomplished without the taking of a single life.

I sat in the high saddle and looked up at the mighty

gates of old Farad, where they stood framed between the twin pylons of glistening black marble . . . at the blackly purple sky that stretched above it, powdered with the crystal fire of wintry stars, and the pale, dim orb of the distant sun beyond . . .

Somewhere in that dark vault, faint and difficult to see, the twin moons of old Mars hurtled by in their flight, as they had flown since time itself began.

Mars was mine now, mine and my sons, forever.

Whatever surprises the years ahead held for me, something of me would always be here.

Seven days . . . and in that time, so much had changed, so much had ended. So much had begun . . .

Her fingers were warm in mine, and that warmth would be near me always. To have found a woman to love . . . this too was one of the miracles those seven days had brought to pass.

Nor was it the least of them!

The gates swung wide before me. And I rode at last into my kingdom.